I0592852

Arcane
Awakenings
Books Five and Six

SHELLEY RUSSELL NOLAN

Creator: Nolan, Shelley Russell, author.
Title: Arcane Awakenings Books Five and Six / Shelley Russell Nolan
ISBN: 978-0-6481683-3-1

Subjects: Fantasy fiction

Printed in Australia by Ingram Spark
Cover design: Mariah Sinclair

www.shelleyrussellnolan.com

Also by Shelley Russell Nolan

The Reaper Series

Lost Reaper
Winged Reaper
Silver Reaper

Arcane Awakenings Series

Arcane Awakenings Books One and Two
Arcane Awakenings Books Three and Four

For Dannielle

Contents

Book Five

Divine Captive

1

I scanned the movies on display in the new release section, none of the titles catching my eye. Then I spotted a new edition of an old movie and smiled as I picked it up and turned to face Belinda.

She shook her head, hands on her hips. 'Grace, you can't be serious. You have made me sit through that movie a thousand times, and you have a copy at home.'

'You've watched it with me ten times, tops, and this one is the director's cut,' I said. 'It has never before released footage. Cut scenes and interviews with the cast.' I scanned the back cover. 'It even has a blooper reel. We have to watch it.'

Belinda gave a sigh. 'Any chance we can just watch the new bits and not sit through the entire movie?'

I looked at her, not saying a word.

'If we only watch the new bits, I'll let you pick another movie,' she said with a hopeful smile.

I continued to stare at her.

She rolled her eyes. 'Fine. I will sit through the stupid movie one more time just so you can ogle Liam Devine.'

'Not ogle. Worship. He plays a god in this one, remember? Which I must say is very apt casting. He is a god. A yummy and delicious god.'

Belinda shook her head. 'I can't believe you still like the guy. He hasn't put out a new movie in years.'

'Once a god, always a god.'

After yet another sigh and shake of her head, Belinda

turned her attention to the rest of the movies. On our Friday night movie sessions, we got to pick one each. Seeing as she'd let me get away with choosing an old title, I didn't complain when she picked up a sappy romantic comedy and started reading the back of it. I preferred action movies with lots of snappy dialogue and explosions. I'd have been more than happy to watch *God Unleashed* twice in a row, no matter that I probably had seen it a thousand times.

Not just to ogle Liam, as Belinda had suggested. It was a good movie, with everything I liked. It was just made that bit better by having my favourite kind of eye candy in it.

'He truly is divine,' I said, staring at Liam Devine's image on the front cover of the DVD case as Belinda continued to browse.

'According to the tabloids, the guy turned into a recluse after the stampede at the convention last year,' said Belinda. 'You're never going to meet him if he doesn't come out of whatever cave he's hiding in.'

Belinda was right. He hadn't been seen in public for months, and there'd even been talk he was in rehab somewhere, but I didn't believe everything that was printed in the gossip magazines. Even if he hadn't become reclusive, the chance of him showing up in Easton and falling madly in love with me were slim at best, but it never hurt to dream.

'I'll get to meet him in person one day. His last name is Devine. Too similar to D.I.V.I.N.E to be a coincidence. And my name is Grace. I'd be the perfect match for him.'

Belinda snorted. 'Grace Devine does have a nice ring to it, I suppose.'

No sooner had she spoken than she stiffened, eyes going wide.

I clutched her arm, holding her steady as whatever vision she was having took over. I'd seen enough of these in the weeks since she'd moved back into the flat with me to know what was happening. As I continued to support her, I fished my phone out of my bag with my free hand, ready to call her boyfriend, Scott Carlton, so he could swing into action as soon as he had the details for whatever catastrophe was about to hit.

After a long moment, the tension in Belinda's body eased and she gave herself a shake. 'It's okay, you don't need to call Scott.' She pointed to my phone. 'This vision was about you.' Her brow furrowed.

'Me?' My voice squeaked, hoping it wasn't bad news. But all of her visions dealt with one drama or another. My heart thudded in my chest.

'Am I going to die?'

'What? No. It wasn't that type of vision. This one was different. Weird. Almost like I was watching a movie. One that starred you and Liam Devine.'

'Is that right?' Eyes narrowed, I crossed my arms and waited for her to tell me what she'd seen. I was surprised it'd taken her this long to come up with a "vision" to trick me.

'Like I said, it was weird. I got a glimpse of the two of you standing side by side, holding hands, wearing purple robes. You were addressing a bunch of people all dressed in white. They were kneeling in front of you. It looked like they were worshipping you both.'

'Belle, that's not nice. Teasing me like that. So what if I have a crush on a former movie star. It's not like I have a handsome police officer to keep me warm at night, like you do. I'm allowed to dream about being swept off my feet, without you making fun of me, regardless of how far-fetched it might be.'

Her cheeks flushed. 'I'm not making this up. I seriously saw you and Liam Devine, and it sure looked like you were

5

being worshipped.'

I pulled on her arm, shaking my head. 'Just hurry up and pick your movie, before I choose another one with Liam in it just to annoy you.'

Moments later she made her choice and we moved over to the front counter and waited for the attendant to scan our movies. After a quick stop to pick up our takeaway order from *The Curry House*, we headed home.

Scott called Belinda while we were halfway there, and I got to listen to their barely disguised love talk for the rest of the drive. Not that I begrudged her having a boyfriend. I just wished I wasn't in earshot while they made up for spending a night apart.

This was the first movie night we'd had for some time, and it was only because Scott was off on assignment for the taskforce he was part of. I hadn't been given all the details, but he'd been handpicked because of his involvement in the case where Belinda had been kidnapped by a crazy scientist who planned to use her ability to see the future for some nefarious business.

For a girl who claimed all she wanted to be was an artist, my best friend was doing a good job of turning into a super hero. As well as assisting the police in the search for the crazy Dr Frankel, she liaised with the taskforce via Scott, letting them know what she saw in her visions, so they could stop bad things from happening. Seeing as I had no psychic ability and was also not a police officer, she wasn't authorised to share most of the details with me, but I'd heard enough to know freaky stuff had been happening in Easton over the past year.

People infected with a weird virus had gone crazy, attacking people before collapsing and dying. After that there'd been a lockdown instituted while a private security force took to the streets when what was reported as gang rivalry got out of hand. I hadn't paid much attention to the reports as it was just after the car accident that'd blinded Belinda, but I'd since heard rumours the gang situation was a cover-up for something more sinister. It was around that time when the taskforce Scott now worked for was created, so I wouldn't be surprised to find out the rumours were true.

With all that had happened, I was just glad Belinda's involvement in the taskforce was being kept secret. Once the initial interest in her visions had died down, with no new leaks to the press, she had been able to work in the background, letting the police be in charge of that aspect. So, life was mostly back to normal for Belinda and me. She had returned to university to finish her Arts Degree, while I got to play with cute and cuddly animals in my job as a receptionist at a vet surgery.

By the time I pulled into the driveway of the small flat we shared Belinda had finished her conversation with Scott, and we settled down to eat our dinner and watch the first movie. I graciously let Belinda go first. She'd picked the romantic comedy, which I had to admit was pretty good. Not at all sappy like I thought it would be.

Then it was time for my movie, with explosions, car chases, and Liam Devine. Belinda didn't complain while we watched it, though I caught her rolling her eyes a few times. Yes, it was weird having an action adventure with a pro-surfer who finds out he is actually a teenage god from another dimension. He turns out to be able to control water and has to use it in ingenious ways to fight off the bad guys intent on stopping him from returning to his home world.

But hey, if I got to ogle Liam Devine then it was all good. Especially the scenes where he took off his shirt to display the toned muscles he was blessed with. With these, combined with his topaz eyes and shoulder length blond hair, he definitely looked the part of a surfer god. It helped that he surfed in real life, so he was able to do most of the stunts himself, as evidenced by the extra material Belinda sat through with me.

It had been a long week, with a number of late nights at the surgery, so by the time the final extra scene had played I was finding it hard to keep my eyes open. With matching yawns, Belinda and I headed off to bed. It felt like I had just closed my eyes when I was woken by a loud thump outside my bedroom window. It was accompanied by a low *whuff* noise, and I groaned.

'Damn it, Harold. You better not be rummaging in our bin again.'

The neighbour's dog, a huge beast that looked like a cross between a Wookie and a polar bear, made a habit of escaping his own yard and coming to play in ours. But his kind of play usually involved tipping our rubbish bin over and investigating the contents, leaving us with a backyard strewn with rubbish.

I got out of bed and padded over to the window. But when I looked outside there was no sign of Harold, though the bin was on its side with rubbish bags spilling out from it.

I heaved a sigh, knowing I'd have to put the bags back in the bin and stand it up before the dog returned to finish the job. I stepped into the hall, looking toward Belinda's room. There was no light showing under the door, so she must not have heard the bang. She often had disturbed nights, thanks to her visions, so I wouldn't wake her for something as trivial as this.

I slipped out the back door and headed over to the bin to right it. I leaned down to grab the closest bag of rubbish, glad we used sturdy bin liners and tied the ends, so nothing would've fallen out. As I reached down to grab a second bag, a noise came from behind me.

Sure it was going to be Harold, I prepared to use my most gruff voice to send him packing as I turned around. He was a big lug, gentle as they came despite his hefty size. From experience I knew he would look at me with his big puppy dog eyes and try to wheedle his way out of trouble, but I had plenty of experience dealing with wayward canines.

Only it wasn't a dog standing in front of me.

A tall figure, clothed head to toe in black, stared back at me, features in shadow. My heartbeat sped up as I struggled to figure out who he was and what he was doing there. He stepped closer, the light from the back door allowing me to see he was an older man with dark hair and eyes.

Before my brain had a chance to process his sudden appearance, he lunged forward and grabbed hold of my arm, pulling me toward him. I dropped the bag of rubbish and hit out at him even as I opened my mouth to scream. But he covered my mouth with a gloved hand, a cloth wadded up in his palm. A bitter scent wafted in the air, like the anaesthetic we used at work, and I held my breath when I realised the cloth was soaked in chloroform.

With my mouth and nose covered, I couldn't take a breath without risking being rendered unconscious. But I wouldn't be able to hold it for long. I wrenched my body sideways in an attempt to dislodge him. But he was strong, so much stronger than me.

I kicked back at him, hitting his shin, wishing I was wearing boots so it could do more damage, but all he did was grunt and hold me even tighter. Head reeling, running out of oxygen, I made one last effort to get free. I jabbed him in the gut with my elbow, putting as much force as I could in the blow.

It worked. His grip around my waist loosened. I ripped the hand with the cloth away from my mouth, sucking in a lungful of air ready to scream the place down.

He pointed at me and even though he wasn't touching me my throat constricted, cutting off my scream. It felt as if I had his hands wrapped around my neck, but that didn't make sense. He had to be doing something to me. The only sound I could make was a faint gurgle. He increased the pressure and my vision wavered. I spun around, movements jerky as I tried to get to the back door.

I had to get inside. Lock him out.

My vision darkened as oxygen deprivation kicked in. I felt my body fall, dimly registering that whatever had gripped my throat had let go. But it was too late. Hands gripped my body and I was swung over a shoulder before falling into complete darkness.

2

I came to, gasping in air as the memory of being strangled hit.

I froze, hands halfway to my neck, and gaped at my surroundings. I was sitting in the middle of a huge four poster bed, purple velvet curtains trimmed in gold pulled back and tied to each post. Gauzy curtains were down, obscuring my view of the rest of the room, but what I could see was just as unfamiliar as the bed.

Where the hell was I?

Heart pounding, breathing hard and fast, I thrust the curtain aside and climbed off the bed, head swivelling to take everything in as my feet sank into plush carpet. I ran my hands over my body, some of my panic easing at the discovery I was still wearing my pyjamas. I was also sporting a number of aches and pains. However I'd got here, it had left bruises. The worst was my throat. It hurt both inside and out from what my attacker had done to me. All without touching me.

I sucked in a ragged breath, wincing as it burned on the way down. Whoever he was, he had psychic abilities like Belinda, who had been kidnapped twice because of it.

Dread pooled in the pit of my stomach at the thought the man who had kidnapped me could be working for Dr Frankel. Belinda had said he had a young guy working for him who could also see future events. I had only caught a brief glimpse of the man who attacked me, but he had to be in his mid-forties at least. So he couldn't be the same guy who had been after Belinda.

Of course, that didn't mean he wasn't working for Dr Frankel.

But, if that was the case, what did he want with me? I didn't have psychic abilities.

Unless... He'd thought I was Belinda?

Relief swamped me, to be swiftly followed by horror.

This new guy must have got me mixed up with her.

I had to get out of there. Had to warn Belinda that Frankel was after her again.

I spotted a door on the other side of the room and ran toward it, feet making no sound in the thick grey carpet. I wrenched open the door and my eyes widened. It was a huge walk in wardrobe with one side filled with white dresses with long flowing sleeves. Hanging alongside the dresses were a number of dark purple velvet robes with gold trim around the collar and hem. On the floor below them sat ballet flats, the same colour as the robes, in various sizes.

On the other side of the wardrobe were more robes and shoes, in larger sizes, and what looked like white pants and tunic styled tops. Definitely men's clothing.

At the end of the wardrobe I could see a sliding door that was partially ajar, letting me glimpse white tiles and a basin. I stepped closer and slid the door fully open, finding a luxurious bathroom with a huge clawfoot tub sitting in pride of place, a glass walled shower cubicle and a toilet partially hidden behind a partition.

Head buzzing with everything I'd found, I headed back to the bedroom in search of a way out. My breathing was shallow, fast, and I fought to calm myself as I scanned the large room. There were no windows, the only light coming from bulbs set in heavy brass sconces on the walls.

There was another door on the opposite side of the room and I ran over to it, cursing when I found it was locked from the outside. There was no way out. I was stuck, at least until whoever kidnapped me came back and I could tell them they'd made a mistake.

But what would they do, once they realised I wasn't Belinda?

There was a spacious sitting area opposite the door, with a grey couch pushed against the wall and a dark mahogany coffee table in front of it. I shuffled over to the couch and sat down to watch the door, both willing it to open and dreading what would happen when it did. My gaze skimmed the objects on the coffee table, noting a tray in the middle with a water jug and two glasses set out on it. But it was the folded piece of paper in front of it that caught my attention.

The side facing me had a name written in neat handwriting on it.

My name.

Hands shaking, I picked up the piece of paper and unfolded it, staring in horror at the words written inside.

Clothes have been provided for you. Ensure you are dressed and ready for inspection when I return. Do not disappoint me. It will not end well for you should you choose not to do as I have requested.

I scrunched up the note and threw it on the ground, using anger to push back the panic threatening to overwhelm me.

Who the hell did he think he was?

There was no way I was putting on any of the clothes he'd provided for me.

No way.

I crossed my arms over my chest and glared at the door, waiting for him to show his face so I could blast him, trying not to think about the fact it was my name on the piece of paper, or that I was sitting in what could be termed a luxurious jail cell; one that contained clothes for a man as well as a woman.

He hadn't thought I was Belinda. He'd known who he was kidnapping.

But that made even less sense.

I sat there for half an hour at least, unable to gauge the time without a watch or clock. Eventually my bladder demanded I move. When I came out of the bathroom, drying my hands on my pyjama pants as I walked back to the couch, I froze halfway there.

The door was opening.

I raced across the room, ready to escape this bizarre prison, only to screech to a halt when a figure dressed in white pants and a tunic top the same as what was hanging in the wardrobe entered the room. He slammed the door closed behind him, blocking it with his body.

Tall, with brown hair lightly tipped with grey, I wouldn't have given him a second glance if I passed him in the street, except for the forbidding look in his hazel eyes as he glared at me. There was no doubt in my mind that this was the man who'd attacked me in my own backyard.

'I told you to get dressed,' he said, anger filling his voice.

I tossed my hair over my shoulder and glared at him. 'Who the hell are you? Why have you brought me here?'

He waved his hand and I was pushed backward, legs scrambling to keep me upright. After a few steps the backs of my knees rammed into the coffee table. I sank down onto it, head reeling as he crossed his arms in front of his chest and stood there staring at me.

'Get dressed,' he said.

Stamping down hard on my fear, I got to my feet, fists clenched at my sides, hoping he couldn't tell how much I was shaking. He'd pushed me back, without touching me. Just as he had practically strangled me the night before. As much as I hated to give in, I turned my back on him and hurried into the wardrobe, rummaging through the clothes on the left-hand side for a dress that was my size. I found a selection of white underwear on a shelf and hurriedly found some that would fit. Then I headed into the bathroom to change.

The bodice of the dress hugged my torso while the full skirt fell to the floor, swirling around my feet with each movement. There was a large mirror above the vanity and I stared at my reflection, not comfortable with the way the scooped neckline showed off my cleavage, or how the white of the dress contrasted with my tanned skin and long black hair. Hair that was a tangled mess.

To delay the moment when I would have to face my kidnapper again, I hunted for a brush in the vanity drawers, and for something to tie my hair back with. Hands shaking, I found a brush, an unopened tube of toothpaste and a two pack of toothbrushes. I freshened up, but with no hair ties or pins I had to leave my hair down.

After one last glance in the mirror, sure the panic threatening to overwhelm me was visible in my grey eyes, I took a deep breath and left the false security of the bathroom. It was time to get answers.

The man who'd kidnapped me stood in the same position as when I'd left, and he gave an approving nod when he saw me.

'Much better. Now you look the part. Although, when you leave this room you will wear the robe, and the matching shoes. You are not to appear in public without them.'

A shiver swept over me at his words about looking the part, legs threatening to fold beneath me. Had he brought me here to live out some sick fantasy of his?

I stiffened my spine, determined not to let him see how scared I was. 'What do you want with me?' My voice shook despite my effort to keep it steady.

'There's no need to be afraid, Grace. In time you will come to appreciate all that I offer you.'

'You haven't offered me anything. You kidnapped me.' My hands went to my throat, vividly remembering how it felt to be strangled with ghostly fingers, to be pushed backward by a wave of his hand.

'My name is Mark Davidson, and I apologise if my initial approach frightened you, but I couldn't take the risk you would choose not to become part of the Order.'

'The Order?'

'The Order of the Arcane. An organisation formed to protect people like you and me. Recent events in the world beyond this sanctuary have proved those of us with psychic abilities have become targets. The Order seeks to prevent that happening, which is where you come in. You, and Liam Devine, will become the face of the Order.'

I flung up my head, eyes wide. 'What did you just say?'

'It's time those who would use our abilities for their own gain learn that we are the superior race. We are the ones who should be in charge. Once Liam arrives, we will begin our campaign to wrest control of the country from those who do not deserve to lead. The two of you will be our figureheads, the ones the public will come to revere and worship.'

I gulped down bile.

Belinda's vision of Liam and me, hand in hand, wearing purple robes while people dressed in white knelt before us.

Oh. My. Freaking. God.

'You're insane. I'm not going to be a figurehead for some lame religion.' Shaking my head, I backed away from him. This could not be happening.

16

'It will happen. The seers have had visions of it. You will be the Goddess to Liam's God. Together you and he will lead our Order to greatness.'

My body shook, and I wasn't sure if it was from anger or shock. 'I'm telling you, your seers are wrong. I don't have a psychic ability. I'm just an ordinary girl.'

Mark clearly thought Liam Devine also had an ability, which had to be crazy. He was an actor. Former actor. But then, Belinda had been normal until her car accident. A lump appeared in my throat at the thought a new-found ability could explain Liam's decision to quit acting and become a recluse.

'Impossible. I saw you, at the video store, communicating silently with your cousin,' said Mark, brow creasing.

Eyes wide, I pushed back the realisation that he'd been watching us. 'We've been best friends as well as cousins our whole lives. We know each other so well we can hold entire conversations without words, but I'm not telepathic.'

He stepped closer and I tried to dodge, but he froze me in place with a wave of his hand. Body rigid, unable to move, tears of frustration leaked from my eyes as he grabbed hold of my head, his gaze boring into mine.

After a tense moment he let go and stepped back, shaking his head. 'I knew I should have stuck to the original plan and taken your cousin. But after I heard her recount her vision to you, I changed my mind. She is, by all reports, a very powerful seer. Taking her vision into account, I acted accordingly.'

It took a moment for his words to sink in. Then it hit. He'd intended to kidnap Belinda, but her vision had made him change his mind and take me instead.

Cold sweat enveloped my body.

He wasn't going to let me go.

17

Unless I could convince him he was wrong.

Even if I was successful in escaping, he might go after Belinda. She'd been his original target. She'd been through so much, terrified she was going to lose her eyes when Dr Frankel had her. I would not let Mark Davidson hurt her.

But how was I going to stop him?

3

To buy time to think, I went on the attack.

'That is the most ridiculous thing I have ever heard. As if someone like you would ever be able to run the country. The authorities will send you packing the minute you try to take over.' Hands on my hips, I shook my head. 'You are clearly certifiably insane.'

His face went so red as he shook a fist in front of my face, I thought for sure he was going to hit me. But then he got himself under control and took a step back.

'Our seers may not be as powerful as Belinda, but after I brought you here two of them inspected you and confirmed you would be the best mate for Liam. You must have a psychic ability. It just hasn't awakened yet. For some people it takes a traumatic experience before their abilities manifest.'

I screwed up my mouth, squirming at the thought of his "seers" inspecting me while I was unconscious. 'A traumatic experience, like being kidnapped by an idiot who bases his decisions on things he heard while eavesdropping?'

Face flushing once more, nostrils flaring, he loomed over me. 'What's done is done. You are to be Liam's mate. With training, we will awaken your abilities. In the meantime, you are to tell no one that you do not possess an ability as yet.'

I tossed my head, glaring at him. 'I'll tell them. If you don't let me go, I'll tell every single one of them this is all a mistake, that you're a fraud, and this Order of yours is bogus.'

He gave me a grim smile. 'Once Liam arrives, if you truly do not have a latent ability he will be able to compel you to obey me. You will do anything he tells you to and believe it is your own will guiding you. You and he will usher in a Golden Age for the Order of the Arcane.'

'You can usher in your own Golden Age. I don't want anything to do with you or your Order.'

'What you want is immaterial,' he said, lips forming a smirk. 'One way or the other you will be at Liam's side as he tours the country, compelling all those without an ability to follow the Order. Anyone who is not psychic will fall at his feet, and once we have sufficient numbers we will be able to seize control. You should be glad to know that one day your children will be born into a world where they will be viewed as gods and will continue to build on our legacy.'

A day ago, the idea of having Liam's babies might have filled me with glee. Now the thought he might have the ability to coerce me into doing whatever he wanted made my stomach churn. It was hard to fathom how my favourite movie star could be part of something like this, but the conviction in Mark's voice put a dent in my scepticism.

But that didn't mean I was going to sit there and let anyone, even Liam Devine, brainwash me into believing any of this was real. I had to escape, find Belinda, and keep her safe while Scott's taskforce took care of Mark and his Order. I just hoped this was the kind of thing they were equipped to handle.

As these thoughts ran through my head I reached behind me for the jug of water, snatching it up and tossing it at Mark in one movement. He ducked to avoid getting hit in the face and I bolted for the door, hoping he had left it unlocked. A hard shove in the middle of my back sent me reeling. I slammed into the door, head connecting with the unyielding surface. Another shove pushed me sideways and I fell to my knees, vision blurring as legs appeared in front of me.

A moment later I felt myself being lifted in the air, before bouncing down in the middle of the bed. A cloth with a familiar scent was placed over my face.

Dizzy, nausea bubbling away in my stomach, I was unable to stop myself from breathing in. My eyes closed as I dimly registered the removal of the cloth and the slamming of the door.

The pounding in my head pulled me back to reluctant consciousness, and I groaned as I rubbed my temples. My stomach recoiled at the thought of moving, so I lay there, waiting until the nausea had subsided enough for me to sit up.

With a bunch of new aches and pains riddling my body, I dragged myself to the door and discovered I was once again locked in.

Still lightheaded, I crossed over to the couch and sat down, leaning back with a soft groan. The jug of water I'd thrown at Mark was back on the coffee table, refilled. A wet patch of carpet showed where its previous contents had fallen. A plate with a dome shaped cover over it sat beside a thermos flask, a coffee mug, a sugar bowl and a milk jug. I lifted the cover off the plate to reveal a chicken and salad sandwich cut into four neat triangles, and my stomach rumbled. I hadn't eaten since the takeaway curry the night before and had no idea how much time had passed since then.

I quickly demolished the sandwich, washing it down with water.

Having food in my belly helped with the nausea, and the pounding in my head had reduced somewhat as I inspected the contents of the flask. Coffee, strong and black, just the way I liked it. I filled the mug to the brim and inhaled the rich scent, enjoying the way the smooth liquid slipped down my throat. I'd just finished my coffee, and was contemplating

21

pouring myself a second one, when the door to the room opened.

Mark stepped inside, and I stood, preparing to yell at him for drugging me again, but he waved his hand and my throat constricted. I sank back to the couch, struggling to breathe as four men dressed in identical white pants and tunics carried a plain wooden coffin into the room and set it on the ground beside the bed.

If I hadn't already been fighting for breath, I would have been hyperventilating at the sight of the coffin. Had he changed his mind? Was I going to be killed and then tossed in the coffin and buried? Would he then set his sights on Belinda once more?

I hunched over, coughing as my lungs sought more air. Mark waved his hand and the pressure on my throat lessened enough to make it possible for me to suck in small amounts of air, but I still couldn't talk. I straightened up, watching as he pried the lid off the coffin and set it aside as two of the men leaned in. A moment later they picked up a still figure from inside the coffin and placed it on the bed.

It was a man, and my heart thudded in my chest as I saw wavy blond hair and a familiar face.

Liam Devine.

The four men left the room, taking the coffin with them, and the pressure on my throat vanished.

Mark looked over at me. 'Take care of him. The drugs he was given to ensure his cooperation will wear off soon. I will have more food brought to you and then I will return tomorrow to begin instructing the both of you in what your roles in the Order will entail.'

He left, and I heard the click as he relocked the door. But I stayed where I was, staring at the still figure on the bed.

What the hell was I supposed to do now?

Hands shaking, I pushed my hair back from my face and approached the bed, staring down at the man I had never dreamed I would one day meet in person.

Scrapes and bruises could be seen through tears in what had once been a nice shirt, and dried blood was visible on his face and knuckles. There was also blood on his cargo pants, and he seemed to have lost his shoes at some time during his journey, though he had managed to keep his black socks on.

What was he going to do? How would he feel and react when he woke and realised what he'd been dragged into the middle of? If the state he was in was any indication, it appeared Liam was no more interested in being a figurehead for the Order of the Arcane than I was, even if it was true that he had some kind of psychic ability.

I turned away from the bed and headed to the bathroom where I found an enamel bowl in a cupboard beside the vanity and half filled it with warm water. The cupboard also contained clean towels and I grabbed one as well as a face washer. Then I took it all back to the bedroom.

Perching on the side of the bed, I placed my supplies down on the other side of Liam. As I undid the few remaining buttons of his torn shirt, I winced once I got a better look at the extent of his injuries.

'Well, it certainly looks as though you put up a fight. And, judging from the state of your knuckles, I'd say you landed a few punches yourself. Good for you. I only hope whoever did this is hurting even worse than you are.' As I talked, I gently washed away the dried blood on Liam's face, hands and chest as best I could. I didn't want to press too hard and risk hurting him.

The door to the room opened and I looked up as the men who'd carried the coffin in entered the room. Two of them remained at the doorway as the others placed a number of items down on the coffee table, all without making a sound. I waited until they'd left to check Mark had been true to his word. A second thermos flask was on the coffee table as well as another coffee mug and a number of covered plates.

I returned to Liam and dried him off with the towel, and then sat back to admire my handiwork. Running my gaze over his familiar features, I compared the live Liam to the one people saw in the movies and magazines. He didn't look all that different as he lay there. He looked peaceful despite his bruises. His hair was shorter than it was when he starred in *God Unleashed*, and several days' worth of stubble gave him the unkempt look he'd been famous for. His chest rose and fell evenly, body still.

Eyes narrowed, I stared at the surprisingly delicate fall of his dark lashes as they fluttered slightly. 'Okay, how long have you been awake?'

His lashes flickered again in response to my question, but his eyes remained closed.

'Give it up, Liam. I know you're awake, so you can stop pretending. Either that or stop twitching your eyelids.' Shaking my head, I watched as he tried to keep his eyelids still, waiting for him to recognise the futility of his pretence. Maybe he would give it up if I gave him some reassurance.

'It's all right. Mark and the others have gone so it's just you and me here.'

Liam opened his eyes, golden gaze locking onto mine.

I forgot to breathe, body temperature soaring and then dropping just as rapidly as it had risen when I realised what I'd been doing.

I, Grace Ann Evans, had practically undressed and then given a sponge bath to Liam Devine. A guy I'd been crushing on since I'd first set eyes on him in the television drama *Flanigan's Run* six years earlier. He'd been the break-out star, turning the then fourteen-year-old into a heartthrob poster boy for teenage girls all over the country, including me.

I sucked in a shaky breath and pushed all that aside to concentrate on the here and now. 'My name's Grace. I'm sure you have heaps of questions you want answered. Ask away, and I promise to give it my best shot.'

Liam lifted a hand and rubbed his eyes before turning his head and looking around the room. 'Where am I?' he asked, voice harsh from disuse.

He rolled onto his side and tried to sit but fell back against the covers.

I leaned in to help, wrapping my arm around his back and supporting him as best I could. This close, I was conscious of the heat of his body pressed against my side, as well as the strong odour of sweat. There was no telling how long he'd been stuck inside that coffin. He needed to get cleaned up, but not until whatever drug he had been given was out of his system. Giving him a quick sponge bath was one thing, helping him shower was another matter entirely.

A cup of coffee would clear some of the cobwebs in his head, with a bucket load of sugar to soften the shock he was bound to be feeling at the situation he found himself in. With a steadying arm around his waist, I urged him to his feet and slowly led him over to the couch. Then I poured him a coffee and stirred in plenty of sugar, adding milk to cool it down in case his coordination was not up to the task and he spilled some.

His eyes were dull, but after he took a few sips of the coffee his gaze brightened, and he straightened up. He grimaced as the movement no doubt pulled on his injuries, and then put his mug down and faced me.

'Listen, lady,' he said, voice low and rasping, 'I don't know what the hell you and those jerks back on the beach are trying to pull here, but I'm not going to be a part of it. I'm leaving, now, and there is nothing you can do to stop me.'

He sounded pissed off and I couldn't blame him.

He was going to be even more pissed off after he heard what I had to say next.

4

Figuring there was no point in delaying the moment or in taking it slow, I said, 'As I told you before, my name is Grace. Not *lady*. The only way out of here is the door over there, which happens to be locked from the outside, so unfortunately you aren't going anywhere.'

Watching Liam closely, I could tell from the stubborn jut of his chin that he wasn't going to give up just because I'd told him escape was impossible.

'We'll see about that,' he said as he stood. He strode over to the door, and tugged on the handle, body tense.

Liam was in for more rude shocks before I was finished, and I didn't have time to mollycoddle him. He needed to know what was going on before Mark came back to check out his newest acquisition. He may have made good on the promise of more food, but I didn't trust him to leave us alone until the next day.

It was probably best to give Liam all the bad news at once. That way he could vent his anger and emotions now, when it was safe to, rather than when Mark was around to throttle him into submission. I reached up and rubbed my throat, still sore and tender from being half-strangled. Liam had enough bruises without adding more to the list.

He let go of the door handle and stormed back to the couch, looming over me. 'You will unlock that door right now or I will—'

'You won't do anything.'

I scowled at him. He may have been bashed, kidnapped,

drugged senseless and transported halfway round the country in a coffin, but that didn't give him the right to speak to me in that tone of voice when I was just as much a prisoner as he was. I stood and poked him in the chest with one finger.

'What makes you think I can open that door any better than you can? In case you hadn't noticed, I'm locked in here with you. I wasn't given any more of a choice to be here than you were. I want to leave just as much as you do, probably even more. So, if you want to know what's going on I suggest you listen to what I have to say.'

When I was sure I had his full attention, I sat back down and spoke in a more reasonable tone. 'I know you are confused and angry but shouting at me isn't going to solve anything. Please, have a seat and let me explain.'

Conflicting emotions flashed over his face, his body rigid as he glared down at me. Then the fight went out of him and he slowly sank onto the couch, cradling his head in his hands.

'I don't know where we are, but I think it's somewhere near Easton.' Unless I'd been unconscious for longer than I thought, we couldn't be too far from my hometown. 'Other than that, I don't have a clue. I was unconscious when Mark brought me here.'

'Mark?'

'Mark Davidson. He's in charge of this place.' I stifled a grimace. 'He's crazy, thinks people with psychic abilities are superior and should be in charge, and plans to take over the running of the country basically.'

Liam's eyes narrowed when I mentioned psychic abilities, his body stiffening.

'What's that got to do with me? I'm not some psychic.'

'Me either, but that didn't stop him from kidnapping me based on a vision someone had.' I thought it best not to mention it was Belinda's vision that caused Mark to choose me. Or to question Liam's statement about not being psychic. We could get to that later.

'Okay, so he runs this organisation he calls the Order of the Arcane, and his seers supposedly picked the two of us as being the best candidates for acting as the figureheads for when he starts his takeover bid.' Mark could be the one to fill Liam in on the idea that our kids would wind up ruling the country. This was a hard enough subject to broach as it was.

'Mark seems to think you have the ability to compel people to worship you,' I said.

'If I could compel people, I wouldn't have let myself be kidnapped,' he said, with a bitter twist to his mouth.

'From what he said before he brought you here, your compulsion only works on those who don't have psychic abilities. If he's telling the truth, it wouldn't have worked on him and his followers.'

He stared at me, suspicion lighting his gaze. 'Why should I believe you?'

I shrugged. 'Whether you believe me or not, it doesn't change the facts. You and I are locked in here, with no way of getting out without help.'

He continued to stare at me, silent. I lifted my head, meeting his gaze head on, refusing to look away. While I knew he had every right to be suspicious, he had to get over it fast. We were in this together. He had to learn to trust me if we were to have any hope of escaping.

After a long moment he gave a sigh and looked away, running a hand through his hair. A split second later his face screwed up. 'Man, I stink.'

'Yes, you do. The bathroom is through that way.' I softened my comment with a smile as I pointed toward the wardrobe door, figuring he was now alert enough not to fall over and knock himself out while getting cleaned up. 'There are clothes for you to change into on the right. Why don't you go have a shower, and when you're done we can put our heads together and see if we can figure out a way to escape.'

His gaze roamed over my face, as if he was judging my sincerity, before he gave a nod and headed for the wardrobe.

As soon as he was out of sight I poured myself a cup of coffee, sure I would need the caffeine boost to get me through the next few hours.

Locked in a room with Liam Devine. A room with only one bed.

It was bound to be a long night.

Liam's eyes held more of a spark as he came back to the couch, hair wet from his shower, dressed all in white. He picked up his coffee mug and downed the contents in quick gulps as he took his seat.

He gave a shudder. 'Man, that was sweet.' He set the mug back on the coffee table and peeled the covers off the plates.

'You seem in a much better mood,' I said, watching as he crammed a sandwich into his mouth. After his earlier performance I expected him to be all fired up about escaping, not filling his stomach.

'I'm starving. Figured I may as well take care of that while you fill me in on how screwed we are.'

'Very screwed. Mark is telekinetic. He strangled me without even touching me. Twice.'

Liam put down the sandwich he had just picked up, eyes wide. 'Seriously?'

'Yeah, and from what he said all his followers have an ability as well, so getting out of here isn't going to be easy. Especially as we can't even get the door unlocked.'

While he continued with his meal I filled him in on what I knew, which admittedly wasn't much. I was yawning at the

30

end of it, despite the caffeine in my system. With no way of telling what time it was, my body clock was urging me to take a break. Liam's energy seemed to be flagging as well, and I guessed a drugged stupor was no substitute for real rest. But he wore an intent expression as he continued to question me.

'You know this sounds insane, right?' Liam asked.

'Don't tell Mark that. He gets real twitchy when you tell him how crazy he is.' I shuddered, one hand going to my throat.

Liam's gaze followed the movement, and I swallowed heavily when he edged closer. He stretched out a hand, fingers gently stroking the side of my neck.

'He caused these bruises, without even touching you?'

I nodded, not trusting my voice with him sitting so close. He smelled so much better now, fresh and clean after his shower. Though he still wore his stubble.

I cleared my throat and he pulled his hand away, sitting back. 'What about his followers? What kinds of things can they do?'

Before I could say anything, another yawn hit, making my eyes water.

Liam stood. 'I'm sorry, you're tired. I should let you get some sleep.' He scanned the room, and then his gaze swung back to me. 'There's only one bed.'

'Uh huh,' I said, words drying up.

He looked down at the couch. 'I'll sleep here,' he said. 'You can have the bed.'

The couch was a two-seater, and as comfortable as it was to sit on it wouldn't make a good bed for either of us. Eyes fixed on a spot to the left of Liam, I said, 'That's crazy. The bed is huge. There is plenty of room for both of us. Besides, we both need to get a good night's sleep if we want to be able to take advantage of any opportunity to escape.'

Liam gave a slow nod. 'If you're sure?'

'It'll be fine,' I said, aware I sounded anything but sure. But Liam appeared to take my words at face value and headed to the bathroom to get ready for bed.

After it was my turn, and I'd changed into a nightgown I'd found on a shelf in the wardrobe, I headed over to the bed. A flush swept over my body at the sight of Liam stretched out on top of the covers, arms behind his head, his gaze on me.

He still wore the pants he'd changed into after his shower but had removed the tunic top. It was hard not to stare at all the tanned flesh on display, the defined muscles in his torso, the trail of hair, a shade darker than what was on his head, running between his washboard abs and disappearing below the waistband of his pants.

'I wasn't sure what side of the bed you like,' he said, 'so I figured I'd wait for you.'

I cleared my throat, making sure my gaze was fixed on his face and not his naked chest. 'Ah, I usually sleep on the left.' The side he was on.

'Cool.' He slid off the bed and walked around it, slipping under the covers on the right. Then he lay on his side, propped up on his elbow, and watched me.

I hadn't moved, torn between disappointment and relief that he had covered up.

'Pretty sure you can't sleep standing up,' he said, full lips curving into a smile. 'And I promise not to bite.'

I gave myself a shake, dropping my eyes as I climbed into the bed. It was warm from his body heat. I lay on my back, hyper aware of the half-naked man beside me. He was still watching me, I could tell, the weight of his gaze deepening my flush.

I wanted to say something to make it seem less awkward to be sharing a bed with someone I barely knew but couldn't

32

risk tripping over my tongue and making a fool of myself. I'd dated a few guys since I'd finished high school, but none of the relationships had progressed to the stage where we were having sleepovers once I'd made it clear I wasn't interested in casual sex. For me, it had to be a meaningful experience with someone I loved and who loved me back, and I was prepared to wait until I met that person.

Of course, I'd daydreamed about it happening with the man currently beside me, but dreaming was all it ever was. I'd never thought I'd meet him let alone find myself sharing a bed with him.

To be locked in a room with the man I had fantasised about was both exhilarating and terrifying. What if he found out about my crush? I'd be mortified.

No. I had to play it cool. Treat this for exactly what it was. Unforeseen circumstances pushing the two of us together.

I forced myself to meet his eyes. 'Goodnight,' I said, reaching to the switch beside the bed and turning off the lights in the bedroom before he could respond. The light was still on in the wardrobe, the door left open, casting a faint glow over the room as I hunkered down under the covers and attempted to pretend the sleeping arrangements were not freaking me out.

Rustling sounds came from beside me as Liam made himself comfortable.

'Goodnight, Grace,' he said, his voice husky.

Soon he was breathing deep, even breaths and I let the sound of them soothe me off to sleep. But instead of a restful night, I spent the bulk of it dreaming about running through a maze with mirrored walls, all of them showing Liam's reflection, trying to find the real version so we could escape.

When I finally fell into a dreamless sleep, it felt like only a moment had passed before a tantalising scent tickled my nose, gently pulling me back to wakefulness. I pushed the covers back and sat up, looking to the right to see an empty space beside me. Movement in the room brought my attention to the couch.

The lights were back on and Liam stood beside the coffee table, once again lifting covers off plates.

From the smell I guessed we'd been given a hot breakfast. My stomach grumbled loudly in anticipation, though it scared me to think I hadn't heard anyone enter the room to deliver the food.

Had Liam?

I swung my legs over the side of the bed and he looked up and gave a smile.

'Morning. Hope you slept well.'

His gaze was warm, inviting, and I flushed as I pushed my hair back from my face. It was always a tangle in the morning. I must look ridiculous.

'Grace?'

I cleared my throat. 'I slept okay, thank you.' Well, except for the crazy dream of looking for him in the maze of mirrors. My stomach grumbled again, teased by the smells of the food Liam was uncovering.

I slipped out of bed and headed for the bathroom. After tidying my hair, I returned to the main room and accepted the mug of coffee Liam handed me.

'Black, right? No sugar?'

It amazed me that he'd noticed how I liked my coffee the night before, even with everything going on.

'Thank you,' I said, taking a fortifying sip before sitting on the couch. He joined me and there was a companionable silence as we began to eat.

'I'll say one thing for our kidnappers, they aren't being

stingy with the food,' said Liam, a few minutes later. 'They were quiet, too. I didn't even hear them come in.'

I paused, laden fork in front of my mouth. 'Do you think they put something in the food?' For both of us not to have heard them, it seemed suspicious.

Liam frowned as he sopped up egg yolk with a piece of toast. 'I did have the best night sleep I've had in a while, but I don't think it was because of drugs. Not new ones anyway. I just figured my body was still fighting off the ones they stuck in me to get me here. Might be a different story tonight.'

Tonight.

I'd be sleeping in the same bed as Liam again, if we didn't figure a way to escape before then. But that was going to be hard to do if we remained locked in this room all day.

'After he brought you here, Mark said he'd return today to begin our instruction.' I shivered, not sure what kind of instruction would be required for people he wanted to use as figureheads for his fake religion.

Liam frowned. 'I better have a second coffee then, to keep up my strength, and one of these little pastries,' he said, leaning across me to grab a sweet pastry off the plate on my end of the coffee table.

His hair brushed my face as he moved back, and I sucked in a breath when warmth flooded my body at his nearness.

'Sorry,' he said, giving me a wide grin before munching on the pastry.

I ducked my head, hoping my hair hid my flush as I put my fork down on the plate and took a sip of my coffee.

After breakfast was finished, I headed back to the bathroom and got cleaned up. The dress I'd worn the day before was no longer on the floor where I'd left it, and neither were my pyjamas. I changed into a fresh dress, though it irked to not have any real choice in what I wore.

35

When I returned to the bedroom, Liam had already made the bed. He took his turn in the bathroom as I tidied up the empty plates and trays on the coffee table. We'd both had big appetites, probably on account of missing meals while we were unconscious.

After the room was set to rights, there was nothing to do but wait. As the minutes passed with no sign of Mark, my tension grew. I had no idea what to expect, but from what I'd seen so far, I knew Mark would stop at nothing to get what he wanted.

What would he do when he discovered I really didn't have a psychic ability to be awakened?

5

I was on my second cup of coffee when the door to the room finally opened and Mark strode inside.

He stopped in front of the coffee table. 'I trust you both slept well. I have a big day planned, so I am glad to see you have made the most of what we've provided.' He waved a hand over the remains of breakfast.

Liam had been sitting quietly beside me, but now he shot off the couch and bolted around the table. 'Who the hell do you think you are?'

He swung a fist at Mark's head, only to freeze in mid-air, mouth gaping open.

I winced. I'd told him Mark was telekinetic, but I guess he'd had to test it for himself.

'First lesson,' said Mark as he waved his hand and Liam was flung backward. 'You will do what I say, when I say. I'm in charge here, not you.'

Liam regained his footing and stood in front of Mark once more, hands clenched into fists. Worried he was going to launch another ill-conceived attack, I stood and moved to his side, placing a hand on his arm.

Liam glanced at me, some of the tension leaving his body before he focused his attention back on Mark. 'Why are you doing this?'

Mark frowned as he looked over at me. 'Didn't you explain the situation to him?'

I shrugged. 'Guess it's hard to swallow, being told you're going to be the figurehead for some lame arse religion.'

The furrows in Mark's brow creased even more as he glared at me.

Tough. If he didn't like what I had to say, then he should let me go.

'You won't get away with this. The police will be looking for us,' said Liam.

'You have been hiding out in your little beach shack for months, scorning all forms of contact,' said Mark, smoothing down his white tunic top and smiling at Liam. 'No one will miss you. As for Grace, I have people working to ensure her disappearance is not being treated as suspicious. Even if someone did come looking for her, this compound is well hidden.'

It was crazy to think no one would be looking for me, but he seemed convinced of it. What had he done, to make him so sure I hadn't been reported missing to the police? Belinda, for one, would've known something was wrong when she woke yesterday and found me gone. She would've called my parents, and Scott, for sure.

Mark cleared his throat. 'Liam, I brought you here to serve a greater purpose, one that will ensure the future for the Order of the Arcane. Once we go public, with you as our figurehead, all those who have been hiding because of the negative attention their abilities would receive will be sure to join us. In the meantime, I will need you to compel the general masses to comply with my orders, so that we have an army willing to defend us as we take our rightful place in society.'

I bit back a retort but must have made some sound as Mark swivelled to face me, a forbidding expression on his face. After a long pause, he turned back to Liam.

'Once you and Grace are sufficiently prepared, we will announce a tour of the country, visiting each major town and city. I am sure your former fans will rejoice that you have returned to the public spotlight and will flock to see you. As each of them come forward to get your autograph you will apply the compulsion. Once we have sufficient numbers we can begin the next stage of our campaign.'

Liam crossed his arms in front of his chest. 'Your campaign, not mine. I don't want anything to do with it. Anyway, I don't have a psychic ability so kidnapping me was a waste of time.'

Mark's nostrils flared. 'Please don't insult my intelligence. I've been watching you for some time, observing how the fans reacted to your presence during public appearances prior to your shunning the spotlight. At first it was the usual adoration one would expect from teenage girls when faced with a celebrity. But then it became more. You were able to sway them to your thinking. The incident at the convention confirmed it. You're able to order those without a psychic ability to do things, and they are helpless to do anything other than obey.'

'You're crazy. There's no way I can do stuff like that.'

Mark rubbed his chin, eyes focused on Liam, hand obscuring his mouth.

Liam shook his head. 'You can torture me all you want, it still won't make me psychic.'

Mark dropped his hand, revealing a smug smile. 'If you weren't psychic you wouldn't have heard me threaten to torture you.'

Eyes widening, I looked over at Liam and then back to Mark. He'd used telepathy, and Liam had heard him.

While Liam came to grips with that revelation, Mark turned his attention on me.

'From your reaction, it is clear you did not hear me and are indeed "deaf". Which is disappointing. But as the seers still consider you to be the best mate for Liam, I must work with what I have. Only, I need to ensure your cooperation.'

He turned to Liam. 'You will compel her to obey me.'

'No way. I won't do it,' said Liam, hands held up in front of him.

Mark's gaze hardened. 'This is not up for debate. Either compel her to obey me or I will see that she is disposed of.'

Disposed of?

The chilling expression on Mark's face suggested he didn't plan to just let me go.

Eyes wide, I shook my head. 'Hang on, you just said your seers told you I was the best choice.'

'True,' he said, shrugging, 'but you are not the only choice, and I'm sure any vow you make to cooperate would be a lie. This is the only alternative. Either he compels your cooperation, or you disappear, for good.'

He turned back to Liam. 'What will it be? Another death to be laid at your feet or the chance for Grace to live a full and happy life as your partner?'

Liam heaved a deep sigh and turned to face me. 'I'm sorry, Grace.'

I steeled myself, not knowing what to expect as Liam's gaze fixed on mine. I couldn't bring myself to look away even though his eyes were filled with remorse and horror.

Mark gave a satisfied smirk as he said, 'Tell Grace she is to obey me in all things. She will not attempt to escape the compound and will act as a full member of the Order.'

Reluctance coating his voice, Liam repeated Mark's words. I remained still and silent until he was done.

Mark ordered me to face him. 'Grace, pick up that knife,' he said, pointing at the cutlery resting on a plate on the coffee table.

I bent down and scooped up a bread and butter knife.

Mark then said, 'Cut your arm.'

Liam stepped forward, hand stretched toward me, horror wreathing his features as I placed the blade of the knife against the inside of my forearm and pulled it across.

'Stop cutting yourself and put the knife down.'

At Mark's command I stopped and did as he ordered, straightening up once I'd put the knife back onto the coffee table. The knife wasn't sharp, and hardly any blood welled from the cut I'd made, but it still stung.

'Very good, Grace. Now, go and clean that up while I talk to Liam.'

I turned on my heel and headed to the bathroom, quickly wiping my arm and wincing at the renewed sting. There were no bandages in the drawers or cupboard, so I dried the cut with a towel and returned to the bedroom.

Mark was gone, Liam standing alone in the middle of the room with a tortured expression on his face. He stepped toward me, taking my arm and giving a low groan at the sight of the cut.

'I am so sorry. I never wanted to hurt you. But I couldn't refuse him, not if that meant you'd be hurt or worse.' He clutched my hand. 'I wish I could undo the compulsion, but Mark said he'd make you pay for it, if I did. I can't risk you getting hurt.'

A wide smile curved my lips as I said, 'There's no need for you to undo anything. It didn't work.'

He dropped my hand, eyes widening. 'What?'

'Your compulsion. It didn't do anything to me. I just went along with it, so he'd think it worked.'

Liam sank onto the couch, shaking his head. 'But you said you don't have a psychic ability.'

'I don't, as far as I know.'

'What about telepathy? Did you really not hear what he

41

said to me, when he threatened to torture me?'

'Nope. I didn't hear a thing.' I grimaced, remembering the disparaging tone of his voice when Mark had called me "deaf" for not being able to hear his mental voice, as if it was a defect. As far as I was concerned it was a plus.

'Then how did you disobey the compulsion? He was right when he said it forces people to do whatever I want.' His expression darkened. 'I learned that the hard way.'

'What happened, at the convention?' I remembered seeing all about it on the news, how there'd been a stampede and people were trampled in the confusion. A number of them had been seriously injured and one young girl had died.

Anguish floated in the depths of his gaze.

'It's okay, you don't need to talk about it,' I said, wishing I'd never brought the subject up.

He ran his hands through his hair. 'You deserve to know the truth.'

He went silent for a moment and I thought he wasn't going to say anything more. Then he straightened and faced me.

'Strange things started happening about two years ago, after I got knocked out by my own surfboard and a friend had to drag me to shore. At first it was just little things, like people suddenly changing their mind about what they wanted to do when I made a comment. Nothing major, just my friends and others around me reacting to my words in a strange fashion, totally out of character for them. It wasn't until after the convention that I put it together.'

He shook his head, eyes troubled. 'I was signing autographs and posing for pictures, and I was in the zone. You know, all hyped up, pretty damn impressed with myself that all those people had come there to see me. Guess you could say being a teenage celebrity had made my head swell.

42

Anyway, I made some stupid comment about giving a kiss to the girl who proved she loved me best. A real ego boost for me, and I topped it off by saying I wanted them all to prove they were my biggest fan. I was buzzed, my body tingling, but I just put it down to the hype.'

His expression darkened. 'But that's when everything went crazy, all these girls yelling and fighting each other, all of them determined to prove they were my biggest fan. I yelled at them to stop, to get out of there, and this time I felt a giant push coming from me and spreading over the crowd, and the buzzed feeling was ten times stronger. They ran, all of them at once, following my compulsion.'

Gaze fixed inward, he said, 'By the time I realised I'd made them act this way, that they were following my orders, and called out again to tell them to stop it was too late. People were hurt. I stood there, listening to them crying and screaming as the ambulances came and carted the injured away. I knew it was my fault.'

'You didn't know,' I said, moving to place a hand on his arm.

He put his hand over top of mine, giving it a squeeze. 'People kept telling me it wasn't my fault, that it was mass hysteria, and nothing I'd done, but I knew they were wrong. If I'd paid attention all the times strange things had happened around me, maybe I would've figured out something was wrong with me earlier.'

His eyes glistened with unshed tears. 'When the convention organisers told me one of the girls had died I lost it. I took off to my beach shack and shut myself off from the world. I vowed never to hurt anyone ever again. I didn't know what it was I'd done, or how, so I figured the safest place for me to be was on my own. That way I couldn't inadvertently hurt anyone else.'

He gave a harsh laugh. 'I was so determined to never do it again, I didn't even think to use it to stop the guys who kidnapped me.' He shook his head. 'Even now, I don't think I could've deliberately compelled them to leave me alone. But when he threatened you, I knew I had no choice. I couldn't let you be hurt because of me.'

Guilt swamped me, knowing I was the reason he'd broken his vow. Even though it hadn't worked on me for some reason, the fact he'd tried to compel me was clearly eating away at him.

I summoned up a smile. 'You did the right thing, and I'm fine. My arm will heal in no time, and it was worth it to prevent something worse happening to me.'

He clutched my arm. 'You can't let Mark know it didn't work. If he finds out, he'll get rid of you for sure.'

My smile died. He was right. I'd have to pretend to be compelled to obey Mark, which was not a nice prospect. Keeping my face blank as I cut myself with a blunt knife was one thing. There was no telling what else Mark would order me to do, and I'd have to obey instantly.

'Are you sure you don't have an ability?' Liam asked. 'I had no clue there was anything different about me until after that surfboard knocked me out.'

'My cousin, Belinda, is nineteen like me, and she started having visions after she was in a car accident a few months ago. Mark said a traumatic experience can often trigger a latent ability. Being kidnapped is the most traumatic thing to ever happen to me, but I still don't seem to have a psychic ability.'

'Then why didn't my compulsion work?'

Before I had a chance to answer him, the door opened.

Mark had returned, and he wasn't alone.

44

6

A young woman stood a few steps behind Mark. She wore a dress identical to mine and had a petite frame, with soft brown curls fighting to escape a tight bun. Her head was bowed, shoulders hunched as she stared at the floor.

Mark strode forward and gestured at the girl. 'This is Rose. She will be your attendant, Grace. Like you, she has never manifested a psychic ability so is deaf to mental voices.'

He looked over to Liam. 'But there is no need for you to compel her. She is my daughter. Rose will obey me in everything.'

Still watching the girl, I saw her flinch slightly when her father reached around and grabbed her arm to pull her forward.

'Rose, say hello to your new mistress.'

She lifted her head, pretty features forming a polite smile, hazel eyes sombre as she murmured a quiet hello.

I chanced a small smile in response, not really sure what was going on. 'Why do I need an attendant?'

'Rose, and the other girl I have handpicked to attend you, will be the conduit by which others communicate with you. Once you leave this room you are not to speak to anyone, unless I have given you leave to do so. Do you understand?'

I nodded, smoothing my features so he wouldn't know Liam's compulsion had failed.

Mark gave a nod and turned to Liam. 'You will also have two attendants, and the same rules will apply when you are amongst your followers. If you break the rules it is Grace who will pay the price.' Once assured he had made his point, Mark rubbed his hands together. 'I have put plans in motion to bring your chosen attendants here. As they will also be deaf, you will need to compel them to obey me, just as you have done Grace. That way I can be sure there will be no hesitation in following my orders. They will also watch over you and report everything you do and say to me.'

At the announcement that she and the other attendants would be used to spy on us, Rose looked over at me. Her expression was remorseful, hesitant even, and I struggled not to react, to appear as if I was fine with everything her father had said. She then resumed looking at the carpet, so I guessed I'd been successful.

'In other words, these attendants won't want to be here any more than we do,' said Liam, waving a hand toward me.

'True, but that is not my concern. They will become your attendants, and once I have the rest of their friends here they will soon learn this is the best place for them. They will become part of us, despite their failings, while the rest of the deaf will be trained to obey the rule of the Order in all things.'

Mark looked over at me. 'I'm sure you will be happy to know I intend for your cousin to join us.'

Despite myself, I shook my head. 'Belinda won't want to join the Order, and I'm pretty sure her boyfriend will have something to say on the matter too.'

He waved a hand, dismissing my words. 'I am well acquainted with Constable Carlton. He will pose no trouble, and nor will the taskforce he works for. They are even now being diverted away from Easton to deal with a problem I devised for them. He will not be able to interfere when my people retrieve Belinda. Along with Angel, Celeste and Ethan, she will become an integral part of the Order. They will not be given a second chance to refuse my invitation to join us.'

I shivered as he rattled off the names, recognising them as Belinda's new friends, people who had psychic abilities like her. I'd yet to meet them, as Belinda chose to keep that side of her life separate from the rest. But from what she'd told me about them I didn't think they would meekly allow themselves to be kidnapped and forced to join the Order of the Arcane.

I was also sure whatever diversion he'd created to distract Scott would not keep him from Belinda for long. He would do whatever it took to find her, so kidnapping my cousin would be a huge mistake, one we could turn to our advantage.

'Enough talk, it is time for both of you to make your first appearance. Get your robes, and shoes,' said Mark.

Without a word, I turned and walked into the wardrobe to select a purple robe. It was made of thick velvet, weighing me down when I slipped it around my shoulders. Then I rummaged until I found a pair of shoes that fitted. Liam joined me and did the same. He looked over at me and I could see questions brimming in his eyes. We couldn't risk talking with Mark in the room, but I was sure I knew what he was thinking.

This was the first time we'd been allowed outside. We had to be on the lookout for an opportunity to escape, and not be forced to wait for the others to be kidnapped and for Scott to stage a rescue.

Mark led us out of the room, Rose at his side, and we were presented with yet another obstacle to escaping. Four burly guys dressed in identical white pants and tunics waited in the long hallway. I recognised them as the men who'd carried the coffin Liam had been transported in. They stepped in behind us, hard eyes watching our every move.

Mark pointed at two doors set close on either side of a

hallway that ended with the entrance to our room. 'This is where your attendants will stay.'

From the lack of natural light in the long hallway, and the fact he knew the attendants weren't going to be here voluntarily, I guessed these rooms wouldn't have windows either. But there was no time to ponder that. He led us down the hall and stopped in front of a sturdy wooden door. As we waited behind him, he produced a key from a chain hanging around his neck and unlocked the door.

Two of the guards brushed past us and went through the door first, and then Mark followed with Rose still at his side. A not so gentle nudge in the middle of my back from one of the remaining guards set me in motion and I swallowed heavily, not knowing what to expect on the other side.

Liam reached out and grabbed my hand, giving it a reassuring squeeze. I gave him a grateful smile before sucking in a deep breath and stepping through the door.

Eyes wide, I gazed around the enormous room.

Constructed in a dark timber, exposed beams arched high over my head to support the roof. The beams continued down the interior walls, wide windows set between them to allow natural light to flood the space. To the right of the hallway we had come from was a short set of stairs that led to a large stage. The rest of the building was filled with wooden pews like those you would expect to find in a church. A wide aisle ran between them, leading to a huge set of double doors that were open and allowed a glimpse of grass, blue sky and a mass of people all dressed in white.

Mark directed for Liam and me to climb the stairs and then arranged us at the front of the stage. We stood side by side, still holding hands. Rose took a position just behind and to the left of me, while Mark stepped in front of us and gave a nod to someone standing near the double doors.

A stream of people filed inside. They ignored the pews and made their way to the front of the room, eyes fixed on us, all without making a sound.

It was eerie, watching over two hundred people staring at us in silence, with rapt expressions. As the first of them reached the front they lined up in neat rows and went down on one knee, heads down, while those behind them followed suit.

My stomach clenched, recognising this moment from Belinda's vision.

After a long moment, Mark clapped his hands and the people lifted their heads but did not stand up.

'Behold,' said Mark, 'I give you your leaders. Liam and Grace, those chosen to represent us to the world. It will be their task to pave the way for the Order of the Arcane to take their rightful place in society. With them at our helm we will carve out a position as the superior race. All will bow before us and no more shall we be looked down on for having gifts others fear or seek to use.'

He continued on in that vein, firing up his followers. I could see from the fervent looks in the eyes of those kneeling before us that he had them well and truly hooked. But they were his followers. Not mine or Liam's.

All his talk about us being the ones to lead them to greatness was just that. Talk.

For a moment I considered shouting out that it was all fake, a lie, but if I did Mark would know Liam's compulsion hadn't worked on me. So I forced myself to remain silent, conscious of Liam's hand in mine, using the solidity of his presence to comfort and calm me. Whatever happened, I wasn't alone in this.

But it was hard to remain steadfast when Mark started talking about a celebration to mark the joining together of Liam and me. Before I could register what was happening, he turned to Liam and me and held out rings, stating they were to symbolise our joining together in holy matrimony.

I wanted to protest, to run away and hide, but Liam's firm grip kept me in place as Mark performed a farce of a wedding ceremony. It took everything I had not to stumble over the words Mark instructed me to say as I placed one of the rings on Liam's finger and he placed the other on mine.

This wasn't real.

Couldn't be real.

Yet the crowd of people eagerly watching on didn't seem to know that.

With a smirk, Mark announced in a loud voice, 'By the power given to me as High Priest for the Order of the Arcane I now pronounce you husband and wife.'

Loud cheers rang out, the sudden noise terrifying after them being silent so long, drowning out Mark's next words.

His smirk widened. 'I said, you may kiss the bride.'

Heat swamped my body as his words sank in. He wanted Liam to kiss me, here, in front of everyone, as if this was a real wedding.

Oh. My. God.

'And make it a good one,' said Mark, leaning in closer, voice pitched low.

Liam took me in his arms, and I tilted my head back to stare up at him. There was no trace of dismay or distaste at what he was about to do in his gaze. Instead, a smile played around his lips, and he appeared like a husband eager to kiss his new bride. But then, he'd been an actor. Pretending to be something he wasn't had been part of his job.

But for me this was all too real. I was going to kiss the man I'd dreamed about as a young teenager, with hundreds of people watching on. Not only that, I was supposedly compelled to obey Mark. So I'd have to make sure I looked as though this was what I wanted.

The thoughts chasing each other around in my head came to a screaming stop, stilled the second Liam lowered his head and his mouth covered mine. At first the kiss was light, tasting and teasing. But then it became something more when he deepened the kiss. I clung to him, a flame of desire flaring low in my belly when his tongue delved between my lips. I let out a moan, forgetting all about our audience, never wanting the kiss to end.

Dimly, I heard Mark say, 'I present to you, Mr and Mrs Liam Devine.'

The room erupted in a fresh round of cheering as Liam finally released my lips. I stared at him, dumbstruck, all thought of plotting an escape route wiped from my head. I was dazed and confused, and it was a relief when Mark indicated for us to leave the stage and follow him back to our room to be locked away from the prying eyes of his followers.

It was hard to concentrate on what Mark said next, something about leaving us to get accustomed to our new roles, and that he'd return soon to take us on a tour of the compound. Rose followed him out, leaving the two of us alone, but I didn't watch them go, too busy staring at the ring on my finger, the other hand coming up to touch lips still swollen from Liam's kiss.

Holy hell.

I had just fake married Liam Devine.

7

'Grace, are you okay? I had no idea he was going to do that.'

I turned and faced Liam, sucking in a deep breath. He didn't appear to be affected by the kiss, though he wore a worried expression.

I had to keep it together, take my cue from him and act as if that hadn't been the most mind-blowing kiss I'd ever been a part of.

'It's okay. It wasn't a legally binding ceremony. I don't really think I'm your wife.' My face flamed at the thought he would think I'd wanted this, wanted him to kiss me. Fantasying about being with him when he was a distant celebrity was one thing. This was on a level I could never have imagined.

He ran his hands through his hair, and then grimaced as he ripped off the robe. 'This is ridiculous. We have to get out of here.'

'How? If what he said is true, all those people out there have a psychic ability.' That would explain the silence, until the cheering started. There'd be no need for them to talk aloud when they could use telepathy.

'Yeah, I don't think we're going to be able to fight our way out of here.' Liam sank onto the couch.

I hung my robe up in the wardrobe, pleased my heart rate was settling down, and returned to the sitting area.

'Maybe when the others get here we will have more of a chance,' I said, my shoulder brushing against his as I sat on the couch beside him.

'Do you know them?' Liam asked, leaning back, the movement pushing him even closer.

With the heat of his thigh pressing against mine, it took a moment before I was able to focus on his question. 'My cousin has mentioned them, but I don't know them or what they can do. But from what Belinda did say, they managed to get themselves out of some tricky situations. Let's hope they can do the same thing again.'

I twisted the ring Liam had placed on my finger, unaccustomed to the feel of it. It still felt so unreal. Here I was, sitting next to Liam Devine, expected to carry on a rational conversation minutes after we'd been fake married. And I had to pretend a part of me wasn't revelling in his nearness and the memory of his kiss, however it had come about.

Our breakfast dishes had been cleared away, and morning tea had taken its place. I sat and reached for the thermos flask, surprised to find my hands were shaking. It took me three goes to get the lid off.

'Here, let me do that.' Liam took the flask and poured two cups of coffee.

'For a minute there I thought you weren't going to go through with it,' he said as he handed me my mug. 'I thought for sure Mark was going to realise you weren't under a compulsion, but you pulled it off. Not that I think being married to me, in a non-legally binding way, is that bad a deal. The look on your face right now suggests you want to run screaming from the room,' he said with a wry grin.

I managed a smile, determined not to let him see how far off the mark he was. 'You're an actor. You play out roles all the time. Me, not so much. So getting fake married feels all kinds of wrong.' Wrong, in that a part of me wished it was real. But I couldn't let my crush affect my thinking.

'Mark is certainly taking things to the extreme,' I added. 'His kind of crazy is not going to be easy to counter. Those followers of his appeared to be lapping up everything he said to them.'

His expression sobered. 'I know. But it's going to be okay. We will get out of here, somehow. When Mark comes back to take us on this tour of his, we need to be on the lookout for any opportunity to escape. If you think you can get out of here, you need to go. Don't wait for me. Just go.'

I shook my head. 'I won't leave without you.'

He put down his coffee and took my hand. 'If Mark finds out you're not compelled, who knows what he would do. Promise me, if you see a chance, you'll take it.'

'What about you? If I escape, Mark will know for sure that I wasn't compelled. He'll come after you.'

'I'll be fine. He needs me to have any chance of fulfilling his plan. It's you I'm worried about.' His gaze locked on mine, expression determined. 'I mean it, Grace. I want you to promise me that you'll take any opportunity to escape.'

Warmth spread through me at his concern. I gave a nod. 'Okay, I promise. But if I do escape, I'll be back to get you as soon as I can find help.'

He gave me a warm smile, squeezing my hand. 'Deal.'

We stared at one another in silence, still holding hands. There was a light in Liam's topaz gaze, inviting and intent. Then his eyes dropped, and I was sure he was looking at my mouth. I licked my lips, remembering the way he tasted. He moved closer, gaze meeting mine once more, and I was sure he was going to kiss me, for real this time, with no one ordering him to do it.

The door to the room opened.

I jumped, pulling my hand from Liam's grasp as Mark entered the room with Rose and the four guards from earlier.

'Are you ready for your tour, Mr and Mrs Devine?' he asked with a smirk.

Liam stood first, and I scrambled to my feet a moment later.

'Lead on,' said Liam, not taking his eyes off Mark.

After we had put our robes back on, Mark waited for the guards to arrange themselves around us before striding down the hallway and into the church. The church was empty as he led us outside to a large clearing in front of it. It was hot standing in the morning sun while wearing a velvet robe over my dress, but the discomfort was mild compared to the feeling of eyes watching on as we walked through the compound Mark had created to house the Order.

There were a number of demountable buildings on the left of the clearing and I could see people in white doing ordinary chores like hanging out washing or raking leaves. There were even a number of small children sitting on the ground under the shade of a large tree with exercise books on their laps. They were being watched over by two adults. It looked like a school lesson in progress.

'I'm afraid the facilities are not as far along as I would have hoped,' said Mark, pointing to where a crew of workers were constructing a row of two and three storey buildings to the right of the church. 'Our original home was near Sydney, in what used to be a motel, but after it became clear Easton was a breeding ground for those with a psychic ability we decided to move.'

He waved a hand back at the church. 'There are two hundred members of the Order living here at any one time. Others are scattered around the country looking for those who manifest an ability, as well as preparing for the day we begin our campaign.'

I shook my head, unable to believe how many people

there were, and he was saying they all had some form of psychic ability. It seemed incredible. And the part about Easton being a breeding ground.

'Why Easton?'

He stopped walking and faced me. 'At this stage I do not have a solid reason. All I know is that Easton is where many of those with unusually strong abilities are born, such as your cousin and her friends. I was born in Sydney, but my father came from Easton.'

He looked over at Liam. 'I understand your maternal grandmother was from Easton as well. Once this place is up and running completely, and we have done our tour of the country, perhaps there will be time for me to get to the bottom of the phenomenon. For now, it is enough to know that almost every person with psychic ability has some tie back to Easton in their family history.'

It was mindboggling to think my hometown had produced so many of these people. But I pushed that subject aside to focus on my surroundings, looking for any avenue Liam and I could use to escape. Even though I'd promised to go without him if the opportunity arose, I'd much prefer we got out of here together.

I couldn't see any vehicles, but they must have them somewhere. How else would they have all got here? There was no sign of tyre tracks on the grass, so perhaps the vehicles were kept farther back, past the buildings blocking my view. From the lack of traffic noise or anything else to suggest civilisation I guessed we had to be in a secluded spot. It would be much easier for Liam and me to escape in a car than it would be on foot.

'These provide temporary housing until more permanent dwellings can be built,' said Mark, waving a hand at the demountable buildings. Then he pointed toward the building

56

sites. 'Once construction is complete; the compound will be able to house one thousand of the Order's followers. It is here they will learn to control their abilities safely and for the good of the Order.'

A shiver swept over me at the thought of one thousand people with psychic abilities all living in the one place. As crazy as Mark's plan to take over the running of the country had sounded, if he did one day have that many followers maybe it wasn't so far-fetched an idea after all.

We had to get out of here, to stop his plan from coming to fruition.

I wanted to get closer to the construction sites, to see if we could get hold of some tools to use to defend ourselves or fight our way out, but Mark led us through the demountable buildings. We walked to a large square patch of land that had gravel spread over the ground and a number of people in white standing in different areas, awaiting our arrival.

Mark rubbed his hands together. 'Now then, I believe it is time for a demonstration, to show you some of the marvellous abilities we have to call upon in our quest to ensure a bright future for those with psychic abilities.'

The first demonstration involved a man being suspended in mid-air, ten feet high, with no visible means of support, while a woman down below stared intently up at him.

As we watched, the woman stepped back and the man slowly dropped to the ground. Then they switched places and it was her turn to rise in the air. I shared a glance with Liam as Mark ushered us over to where four people stood in a circle around a fire pit. My stomach clenched as they each took turns at setting fire to the branches set up in the pit and then putting them out again.

After that we were treated to another demonstration where over a dozen people were lifting rocks and moving them with the power of their mind. Some of them only seemed to be able to move smaller rocks, while others showed little sign of strain as they hefted ones bigger than me.

It was an impressive display of power, and I could tell from the smug expression Mark wore that he knew it had the desired effect on us.

After the rock throwers had completed their demonstration, Mark led us around the training ground. My gaze fell on a large fence in the distance, a shimmering body of water between it and us. The fence was at least eight feet high, running the perimeter of the compound as far as I could see. Mark led us to the dam to where a group of people were using their ability to shape the water, whipping it up and producing waves.

A road ran on the other side of the lake, heading to a gate in the fence. The other end of the road led to a large shed with three roller doors. The one on the left was up halfway, allowing me to see a nondescript van.

Okay, so we now knew where the transport was and the way out. All we had to do was figure out how to get out of our locked room and make our way here to steal a vehicle and escape without any of the two hundred psychics stopping us. So far, we'd seen people who were telekinetic like Mark, fire bugs and water bugs. What other abilities did they have that we would somehow have to neutralise?

'Being able to throw fire and water around is one thing but taking on the country is another. You're going to need more than that,' said Liam.

'Thanks to you, we will have an army ready to defend us and go where I point them,' said Mark.

Liam shook his head. 'I'm one man. I can only compel so many people, and frankly I'm not sure how useful an army of teenage girls will be. You realise they're the only ones who'll come to see me?'

'You're underestimating yourself. Many of those young girls who idolised you a couple of years ago have grown into young women now, like Grace.'

I squirmed, thinking Mark was going to mention that I was one of the adoring fans who would've screamed and squealed at the sight of Liam four years ago. To be honest, I probably would've done the same if I'd come across him a couple of days ago. No doubt making a fool of myself.

'Besides, the audience will have its share of males and parents, as well as workers at the venues we hire. There will be plenty of recruits for you to compel.'

Liam shook his head. 'I still don't think relying on compelled people to be your army is going to be viable. What happened at that convention was the extreme, a mass compulsion. I don't even know how I did it. Frankly, I'm not even sure if I could do it again.'

'You will do it again. I will make sure of it,' said Mark.

'Your choice, but don't be disappointed if we get there and it only works on one person in the audience.'

Mark gave him a grim smile. 'You would be surprised at just how effective one person could be in spreading our message.' Then he turned and walked off, the guards poking Liam and me in the back to get us to follow him.

He led us back around the dam and over to where the people were still practising their fire skills. Mark ordered them to step back from the fire blazing in the pit, beckoning Liam and me over to him with a cruel light in his eyes.

'Grace, put your hand in the fire,' he said.

I froze for a second, unable to process his words.

Then I stumbled forward, struggling to keep the horror from my face as I moved to do as he ordered, hoping my momentary hesitation hadn't given me away.

'Grace, no.'

Liam lunged forward and stopped me, pulling me back and wrapping his arms around me as I strained to break free to do as I'd been told. I had to make Mark believe I was still under compulsion.

'That's enough, Grace. Stop.'

I went still at Mark's words, stifling a wince at the cold, hard tone he used.

Without another word he stalked off and we had to scurry to keep up with him.

Within minutes we were back in the room, the door locked, with Mark standing in front of us.

'You removed the compulsion,' he said in a deadly, quiet tone, ignoring me to glare at Liam. 'So much for wanting to protect Grace. You've just signed her death warrant.'

8

Mark ordered his guards to strip me of the robe and shoes. I dodged their grasp, Liam darting in to throw a punch at one of them.

Another guard jumped on his back and bore him to the ground, while the one he'd tried to punch went to kick him.

'Not the head,' said Mark, tone still cold and contained. 'We don't want bruises for when we show him to the followers with his new wife.'

Liam roared, trying to buck off the guard on his back and dodge the kick aimed at his ribs at the same time. I heard the air whoosh out of his lungs when the kick landed, but I had my own problems to worry about.

One of the guards had hold of my hair, twisting it in his fist as the other pulled the robe off me.

'It's not her fault. I didn't know I'd undone it.' Liam's voice was a wheeze. 'I haven't used my ability in years, I didn't realise I'd taken the compulsion off her until after it happened. But I didn't tell Grace.'

'What did you say?' Mark put up a hand and waved for the guard holding Liam down to step back.

Liam got to his feet, holding his left side. 'She didn't know.'

'Impossible,' said Mark, brow creased.

'You didn't give her any orders until the fire. That's when she would have realised she had no compulsion to obey you.'

'Yet she pretended to go along with it.' Mark turned to look at me, with a thoughtful expression.

'Wouldn't you? You said you'd get rid of her if she wasn't compelled to obey you. If it was me, I'd have done the same thing.'

Mark was silent for a moment. Then he called out for the guards holding me to let go.

I moved away from them as soon as I was free, darting across the sitting area to stand beside Liam.

Liam wrapped an arm around me and gave me a hug. I resisted the urge to bury my head in his chest. I needed to appear strong. Just because Mark had ordered his guards to release me didn't mean I was safe.

'How did you do it?' Mark asked Liam.

'It was after the wedding. We were talking, and I said I wished I hadn't had to compel her.' Despite his even words, his body was tense beside me. 'Before I knew it, I felt it wrap around her and realised what I'd done.'

'Hm. An act of contrition. Interesting,' said Mark, rubbing his chin. 'We have no one approaching your strength with mental manipulation amongst us. It would appear I have misjudged the amount of control needed to temper your ability. Clearly, where Grace is concerned, your instinct to shield her interferes.'

'I can try again,' said Liam. 'But there's no guarantee I won't accidentally free her from the compulsion.'

'That's fine. We will leave Grace compulsion-free for now.' Mark fixed his gaze on me, eyes as cold as his voice. 'But if I catch you trying to escape or seeding discontent amongst our followers, I will kill you. There can be no opposition to the rules of the Order. Do I make myself clear?'

A shudder ran through my body as I gave a nod, Liam's arm tightening around me.

Some of the coolness left Mark's eyes at my response as he said, 'We will begin work on your control as soon as your other attendants arrive, Liam. When we venture from the compound, I want to be one hundred percent certain Grace is compelled in such a way that an offhand remark from you does not undo it.'

With that he left, taking the guards with him, and Liam and I collapsed on the couch.

'That was close,' said Liam.

I gave a nod, too freaked out to speak. A fresh shudder swept through me at the thought of what might've happened if Mark hadn't believed Liam's version of events. He wouldn't hesitate to carry out his threat to have me killed, of that I was sure.

'Hey,' said Liam, moving closer and slinging an arm around my shoulders. 'It's okay. I won't let anything happen to you.'

I nestled into his embrace, wishing I could believe him.

He was a prisoner, same as I was. But he was the linchpin of Mark's plan. I was expendable. If Mark decided I was no longer useful, I doubted there was anything Liam could do to stop him from getting rid of me for good.

After a long moment, where I soaked up the warmth of Liam's presence, I pulled away and gave him a grateful smile. We remained where we were, side by side, quietly getting to know each other better.

An hour later Rose returned with lunch for us, shadowed by the four guards, before leaving us alone again. It was a repeat at dinnertime.

Being with Liam felt so natural, even if it had come about in the most extreme of circumstances. I was getting to know the real him, not the cardboard celebrity cut-out of my imagination, and I liked what I found.

His concern for my welfare, the way he didn't hesitate to jump in to defend me, and the soft look in his eyes any time he looked at me made me think he wasn't averse to my company either. While I was sure he'd be just as considerate and concerned if he were locked up with anyone else, his intent gaze and the way he kept staring at my lips made me think there was more to it than that.

A delicious shiver had me smiling at the thought he might be interested in me, making me wish even more that we could escape from this prison. Then we could continue to get to know one another without Mark's threats hanging over our heads.

Liam's thoughts must have been travelling in the same direction as mine, as he turned to me and said, 'When we get out of here, I'd like to take you out to dinner. If that's okay with you?'

My wide smile would have told him my answer even before I said, 'I would love that.' I also liked that he'd said when we got out of here and not if. We had to think positive. Planning ahead to a dinner date for when we were no longer prisoners gave me even more to look forward to.

'Great,' said Liam, the hesitancy leaving his eyes to be replaced by a devilish grin. 'But I tell you one thing, I will not be wearing white.' He poked at his shirt, which bore a coffee stain.

I laughed, feeling at ease for the first time in ages. 'Sounds like a plan.'

Liam stood and stretched his arms above his head.

My gaze fixed on the tanned expanse of skin that was exposed by the movement.

'Guess we should be getting to bed,' he said. 'There's no telling what Mark is going to throw at us tomorrow. We need to be alert and ready for any chance of escape.'

The sense of ease I'd experienced vanished as I looked over at the bed I'd share with him for the second night in a row. This early in our relationship, if that was what the attraction between us was developing into, it felt awkward to be sharing a bed. But there weren't a lot of options.

'Hey, relax,' he said, a goofy smile on his face. 'We're married now. We're supposed to share a bed.'

I knew he meant it as a joke, but I still couldn't stop the flush sweeping over my face at his words and all it entailed, pretty sure most married couples didn't sleep side by side with no contact whatsoever. No, far different things, interesting things, happened in the bed then.

Awkward or not, he was right about it being time to get some sleep. I headed for the bathroom to get changed into the nightgown, splashing cold water over my face to get rid of the blush in my cheeks. After I'd brushed my teeth I returned to find Liam had once again turned off most of the lights. He headed into the bathroom and I climbed into bed, glad the darkness would hide my flush.

When Liam returned, I felt the mattress dip as he sat on it. I didn't turn to face him.

'Grace,' he said, voice pitched low. 'You know I was just joking, right? I would never do anything to make you uncomfortable.'

'It's fine,' I said, forcing a lightness into my tone. 'It's no big deal. People share beds all the time, even if they aren't fake married.'

'In that case, fake wife, I just wanted to let you know that I'm glad you're here with me. I'd go crazy if I was locked up in this place alone. Mark may be a nutcase, but I'm glad you're the one he picked to be my partner.'

I didn't know what to say to that, so I just murmured good night. The tension seeped out of my shoulders when he did the same as he climbed under the covers.

It felt even more weird, tonight, with the ring on my

finger even though it didn't really symbolise anything. With all that running through my head, it took me ages to fall asleep, and from the way Liam tossed and turned I guessed he was having the same problem.

It wasn't surprising then, that we both woke when Rose came to deliver our breakfast. As she placed the tray with the plates of food and full flask of coffee on the table she glanced at the men behind her. Then she looked over at where we stood beside the bed.

'Father wishes for the two of you to be fully dressed in one hour. He has collected your other attendants and is on his way here with them.'

I shared a glance with Liam.

An hour. Did that mean wherever we were being held was only an hour out of Easton? After Rose and the guards left, we hurriedly ate our breakfast and got dressed, though Liam grimaced as he put on his robe.

'I feel like an idiot in this thing.'

'Me too,' I said as I pulled mine on and then slipped my feet into the matching shoes.

Liam looked over at me. 'You look amazing in the robe, Grace. Like a Grecian Goddess. Me, on the other hand...' He tugged his rapidly forming beard. 'I look like a loser with delusions of grandeur.'

My mouth opened but I didn't know what to say. He thought I looked like a Grecian Goddess and he looked like a loser. But that was so far from the truth as to be laughable.

'You look just like you did in *God Unleashed*,' I finally managed to say.

'That was the worst movie ever. Don't tell me you watched it?'

I was saved from answering by the door opening. Mark entered first, followed by Rose who had her eyes downcast as usual.

Then three strangers were pushed into the room, two young men and one young woman with long blonde hair. The usual four guards followed them in and the door was shut behind them.

It was a good thing the sitting area was large, with so many people in it. It felt crowded, a hostile environment, especially seeing as the three newcomers were glaring at everyone.

'What the hell is going on?'

'Who the hell are you people?'

'You guys are in so much trouble.'

The three of them spoke at the same time, their words tumbling over one another, making it hard to determine who said what.

'Silence.' Mark paired his order with a wave of his hand and all three of them clutched their throats.

One of the guys swung around, lashing out at the guards, but soon froze in place.

The other guy rushed toward Mark only to find himself lifted in the air, his legs still moving but taking him nowhere.

The girl watched this with a narrowed gaze, before she spun on her heels and bolted for the door. A wall of blue fire blocked her way.

'You can't escape,' said Mark. 'So you might as well sit down and listen.'

The guy hovering in the air dropped heavily to the floor, knees buckling under him. He gave a pained cry and the girl ran to his side.

'Nick? Are you okay?'

'Yeah, I'm good, though a little warning would've been nice.'

The girl glared at Mark. 'Why are you doing this? Is it

because Angel and the others didn't want to join your stupid organisation?'

'Your sister and her friends will join the Order. She will have no choice, now I have you,' said Mark.

'You're kidding, right? You should know by now that they won't work for crazy individuals,' she said.

'They will come to realise being part of the Order is the best use of their abilities. We will keep them safe from people like Dr Wood and Dr Frankel, and anyone else who seeks to use them. But that is something I will discuss with them in time. For now, Andie, it is you who needs to learn who your master is.'

He turned to Liam. 'I need you to compel them to obey me, just as you did to Grace.'

The girl, Andie, swung around to face Liam, wariness in her eyes.

Liam refused to compel anyone, and again Mark said he would dispose of them if that was the case. This time he added that he'd keep bringing people to Liam to be compelled and disposing of them if he continued to refuse, adding more deaths to his tally.

In the end, Liam had to give in. I knew he wouldn't let anyone else die because of his actions.

The guy Andie had called Nick was first. I saw her eyes widen when Liam's compulsion wrapped around him and he immediately stated his loyalty to Mark. Tears filled her eyes when Mark ordered him to hit her and Nick moved to comply.

'Nick, what are you doing? Snap out of it,' the other guy called out, voice frantic as he struggled to get away from the guard holding him.

But Nick didn't answer, didn't stop until Mark halted him when his fist was inches away from Andie's face.

'Now it's Daniel's turn,' said Mark.

I wanted to cry, digging my nails into my palms to distract myself from Andie's horrified expression when Mark again ordered someone she cared about to hit her. Tears streamed openly down her face as he moved to obey.

Mark, a cruel expression in his eyes, let the test of Daniel's loyalty go to the extreme, Andie narrowly missing out on being hit, before he called it off.

'Your turn,' said Mark, looming over her.

Andie kept her head up and shoulders back, refusing to acknowledge Mark as Liam moved toward her.

The two of them faced each other, and as Liam used his ability to compel her to obey Mark I saw her eyes widen before she cloaked her gaze.

I gasped, and then covered it with a cough when I realised what she was doing.

She obeyed the commands Mark gave her to test whether the compulsion worked but there was a slight hesitation, a widening of her eyes that gave her away.

She was like me.

9

Somehow Andie had rejected the compulsion and was only pretending to go along with it. Mark didn't seem to realise, his expression smug as he lined her up with Nick and Daniel and then stood back to survey the three of them.

'This is a momentous day for the Order of the Arcane. Everything I have worked toward for the last twenty years, all the sacrifices I have made, is about to come to fruition. I have travelled all over, searching for those with psychic abilities to build the Order. Now I have the three of you, I will be able to leverage Angel, Celeste and Ethan into joining us freely.'

He turned to face me. 'And I am equally sure Belinda will be pliable once she realises I have her cousin here. If the seers have got it wrong, there is still time for her to take your place as Liam's partner.'

I stiffened, not liking the sound of that at all. Liam was my fake husband.

'Of course, Angel was my first choice. She has multiple psychic abilities, though she is strongest in fire. Her and Liam's children would be unstoppable. Then again, children who could see the future as well as compel those without an ability to do their bidding would be a wonderful addition to the Order. Perhaps it would be best if I bred him with all three of you, to maximise the potential for producing gifted children.'

Okay, that was it. There was no way I was sharing Liam with anyone.

Liam appeared to be equally as horrified as me by the

thought.

Nick and Daniel, on the other side of the room, made no reaction, but I could see Andie's eyes narrow before she caught herself.

Mark continued to go on about his wonderful new idea, talking about getting two more rings and performing further fake marriage ceremonies once he had convinced the rest of his people it was necessary.

That was the last straw. I opened my mouth to say something, to blast him, but Rose touched my arm and stepped in front of me.

'Father, while I am sure you know best,' she said, her voice pitched low and soft, 'you know it is rare for children to display any ability until they reach maturity. But the seers did pick Grace as the best choice for Liam's partner. They did so for a reason, and your followers have taken their vision to heart. They believe Liam and Grace, together, will lead the Order to a glorious future. To suggest now, that the seers were wrong, could undermine their belief in your leadership.'

His top lip curled. 'The seers also chose your mother for me, determining that our offspring would succeed me as the leader for the Order. Instead, we had you. A child with no psychic ability, who would never be accepted by my followers to lead them to further greatness. No, it is much better to hedge my bets, although perhaps it need not be made public.'

He narrowed his eyes. 'You are correct in saying my followers believe Liam and Grace are to lead the way forward. To that end, I will allow them to have one child together. Then Grace will become the surrogate for his children with both Angel and Belinda.'

He smiled over at me. 'Congratulations, Grace. You will become the mother of the future leaders of the world, one way or the other.'

My head reeled from his announcement, revulsion bubbling away in my stomach at the thought of what he hoped to achieve. But I kept that hidden as I waited for Mark and the guards to leave.

Eventually, sick of his own posturing to a group of people who showed little emotion seeing as most of them were either compelled to obey him or were pretending to do so, he left. But he ordered Rose to stay behind to instruct the new attendants on what their roles were to be on a daily basis.

The door closed, and I tried to signal to Andie with my eyes that it was still not safe to talk. Rose would no doubt fill her father in on everything that happened when he wasn't present.

Andie gave me a small nod, saying nothing, and I let some of the tension leech from my body. Nothing short of getting out of there would remove the rest. I turned to Liam, not sure what to say to him that wouldn't make the situation worse or let Rose know that Andie was not under a compulsion to obey her father.

'He is insane,' said Liam, running a hand through his hair. 'We have to get out of here.'

'I can help you with that,' said Rose, her voice stronger than I'd ever heard it.

I turned and faced her. 'Why would you help us?'

She met my eyes, no sign of hesitation or fear in her gaze. 'Because I want you to take me with you.'

Her simple statement rang in the air.

Andie stepped forward. 'How do we know we can trust you?'

'If I was lying, I would have told my father you were somehow not affected by Liam's ability,' said Rose, her gaze fixed on Andie. Then she turned to face me. 'Just as I could've told him that Grace was never under a compulsion to obey him, despite what you made him think.'

'What?' Liam rocked back on his heels.

I shared a glance with Andie and she gave a nod.

'Rose is right. Andie isn't under compulsion,' I said. 'I realised it straight away.' Then I turned to Rose. 'But how did you know it didn't work on me?'

'I realised yesterday, during the meeting in the church, that you were faking your obedience. I knew if Father found out he would dispose of you just as he threatened to do. He is a ruthless man. He wouldn't hesitate to kill anyone who gets in the way of his plans for the Order. Plans I don't agree with.'

'You'd really help us escape?' Liam moved to stand in front of her.

'If you promise to take me with you.'

'Look, no offence, but I'm still not sure we can trust you,' said Andie. 'He is your father, after all.'

Rose's pretty features twisted into a grimace. 'Just because he's my father doesn't mean anything. He hates me. I didn't turn out to be the perfect child, the one the seers promised him. I have no psychic ability. I'm deaf, like Grace.'

She shuddered. 'He's been watching me my whole life, waiting for my ability to manifest. When I turned eighteen, six months ago, without anything happening, still unable to hear the mental voice of him or anyone else, that's when he hatched the plan to get Angel and the others to join. But they refused him, and he knew they were too strong for him to go up against straightaway. The authorities were also on alert, thanks to what Dr Wood had attempted to do.

'So he bided his time, and then Grace's cousin, Belinda, started having visions that came true. That's when he set plans in motion to kidnap her and Liam. But again, with her having

73

a police officer as a boyfriend it made things difficult. He had to wait until he had enough followers loyal to him, so he could create a diversion to lure the taskforce Belinda's boyfriend works for away, before he could act.'

Rose frowned. 'I'm still not sure why he chose to kidnap Grace instead of Belinda, but that was when he put the rest of his plan into motion. We have to get out of here before he becomes so strong no one can stop him.'

Andie moved over to Nick's side. He looked down on her, a blank expression on his face. She cupped his cheek with her hand. Then she turned to Liam.

'Can you undo what you did to Nick and my brother?'

It was Liam's turn to frown. 'I don't know. I've avoided using my ability for so long, I have no idea what I can do with it.'

'You have to try,' I said, moving to place a hand on his arm. 'We can't leave them like that. All it would take is one word from Mark and both of them would turn against us.'

'All right,' he said.

He strode over to Nick and placed his hands on either side of his head, forcing him to meet his eyes. They stayed like that for a long time and nothing appeared to be happening.

Then Nick staggered, pulling away from Liam, hands going to his head. 'What the hell just happened?' he asked, voice slurred.

Andie ducked under his arm and supported him as she led him over to the couch. 'It's okay. Everything is going to be okay now,' she said.

Liam moved over to Daniel and repeated the process, and he joined his sister on the couch as dazed and confused as Nick.

I poured them both a cup of coffee, with Andie instructing me as to how they liked it, and after they'd both taken a few gulps they appeared to be regaining their scattered senses, though careful questions revealed they had no memory of what they had been compelled to do.

In a few short sentences, Andie explained to them what had happened. Horror wreathed their faces when she got to the part about Mark ordering them to hurt her. I was grateful she left out the part about Mark planning to turn me into the mother of Liam's children with other women. Now was not the time to worry about that.

It was time for Rose to fill us in on her plan for how she was going to get us out of here.

We all turned to face her, and she fidgeted under our gazes.

The door to the room opened with a bang, slamming back against the wall as Mark strode inside with at least a dozen men at his back.

'Two of my best people have gone missing, and your sister is a kilometre away from the compound with the others. How did they know where to find us?' He loomed over Andie, reaching out to grab her arm. 'I demand you tell me.'

She pulled free. 'Go to hell.'

The look on his face when she refused him would have been comical in a different time and setting. Her response left him in no doubt that she was not under a compulsion to obey him.

His glare switched to Liam. 'You freed her?'

'I didn't need anyone to free me,' said Andie, hands on her hips. 'You're the dumb arse who didn't think I had any psychic ability and would be able to be compelled.'

Mark's face went red, and then he paled, sucking in air through his teeth. 'You've been in contact with Angel since the moment you came to.'

'Yep. So next time you kidnap someone you might want

to check if they can use telepathy or not.'

He looked as though he wanted to hit her, but he restrained himself, turning with narrowed eyes to face Nick and Daniel. They glared back at him.

Mark rounded on Liam. 'If I can't trust you to obey me, then I will make sure you are surrounded only by those with psychic abilities.'

He pointed at Nick and Daniel. 'Seize them,' he said, and four of the guards lunged forward. Then Mark pointed at me.

'Her as well.'

He faced Liam again. 'I will teach you to disobey me. And don't think for one moment that her friends will save you.' He pointed at Andie. 'My people number in the hundreds. There is nothing they can do to stop me.'

Two of the guards were advancing on me, and I ducked behind the couch as more of them came my way, even as others surged to help those who were trying to restrain Nick and Daniel.

Liam jumped in front of me, fists held up in front of him. 'You're not touching her.'

But there was little he could do against so many, when his compulsion didn't work on them. He was even less prepared to face Mark when he flung up his arm and an invisible force threw him sideways.

He hit the wall and crumpled to the floor.

'Liam, no.' I dodged the arm of the guard trying to grab me, running toward Liam. But a force wrapped around my middle, dragging me backward. I flailed my arms but could do nothing to free myself.

A fist slammed into my jaw, pain radiating through my head and I sagged. I would've hit the floor if a guard hadn't caught me. I was slung over a shoulder, head ringing, my struggles weak and ineffective as I tried to stop them from taking me.

Mark was so angry, I knew he'd have no hesitation in carrying through on his threat to have me and the others disposed of. Rose had just finished telling us how ruthless he was when it came to further the cause of the Order.

As I was carried out of the room, I heard pained cries behind me. It didn't sound as if the others were faring any better than I was.

Then silence came as I was carried down the hall. I lifted my head and saw two guards carrying Nick. He hung in their arms, head lolling, and I didn't think he was conscious. More guards were behind him and I caught a glimpse of Daniel in the same position as Nick.

Of Andie, Rose and Liam there was no sign.

Mark was also not visible, but that was of little comfort.

The guards all had unknown psychic abilities. Nick and Daniel were unconscious, and I had no skills whatsoever to allow me to free any of us.

I had to hope Mark was wrong, and that Angel and the others were able to force their way into the compound before it was too late.

10

The church was empty as I was carried through, the double doors closed.

The guard set me on the ground beside the door while he went to push one half open. I got to my feet, muscles tensing as I prepared to make a run for it. But he stood with his arms wide, blocking the doorway as he advanced on me.

I dodged left and then sprang to the right, but he grabbed hold of me by the hair and pulled me back.

Scalp on fire from the pressure, I shrieked and clawed out at him, desperate for him to let go. He did release my hair, only to deliver a second blow to my jaw.

I staggered backward, in danger of falling to the timber floor of the church. He surged forward and grabbed me, sliding me over his shoulder again. Hung upside down, stunned, I was unable to summon the energy to lift my head as he carried me outside. I closed my eyes, nausea bubbling in the pit of my stomach, losing track of time.

A cool breeze flitted around me, the sun warm on my back. I forced my eyes open and saw a concrete path below me, with neatly trimmed grass to the side of it. The guard carrying me took a left turn and the light grew dim as he stepped inside a building. The ground was concrete, marked with grease and tyre tracks.

It had to be the large shed I had seen the day before. I'd wanted to make my way here but not like this, hanging over a guard's shoulder and without Liam.

I heard a door slide open and was tossed down onto a

hard, cold, metal surface. Moments later Nick and Daniel were tossed in beside me. I tried to sit up, but a rough hand pushed me back down as more people climbed into the back of what had to be some kind of van. It was cramped, dark when the door slid closed, and with a guard holding me down it was hard to see what was going on.

There was no noise in the back of the van, telepathy meaning the guards had no need to talk aloud. I couldn't hear anything from Nick or Daniel either though, and that was not a good sign.

The engine started, a rumble going through the floor of the van, and then I felt it move. Where were they taking us?

I craned my neck and saw two guards were in the back of the van with us. One of them pinning me down, and the other sitting between Nick and Daniel. He had a hand on both their heads, his eyes closed and a crease furrowing his brow.

Was he keeping them unconscious? Was that his ability?

One of them, I couldn't tell which, began to moan. Then Daniel attempted to push himself up. The man with a hand on his head flicked his wrist and Daniel scurried into the corner of the van, eyes filled with horror, hands up in front of his face as if to ward off an invisible threat. Nick started to stir, and the same thing happened to him.

It was crazy, seeing them wedged into the front corner of the van, cowering as some unimaginable horror played out in front of their eyes. It had to be the guard's doing. His hands were up, one pointing at each of them.

The guard pinning me down moved, the pressure on my back easing. Keeping my movements slow, I pulled my hands in under my chest and braced myself. When Nick gave a low moan, and scuttled to the other corner of the van, the guard shifted position. The second I felt his knee leave my back I sprang up, knocking him aside as I surged toward the guard who was somehow torturing the others.

That guard narrowed his eyes and pointed at my head and I flinched, expecting to be thrust into a nightmare.

But nothing happened. I collided with him and he slammed against the side of the van, grunting.

I heard shouting behind me and spun around to see Daniel and Nick shaking their heads, eyes no longer filled with horror.

The other guard flung up his arms and I felt a wave of air push against me, but it was weak in comparison to what Mark had thrown at me. It had little effect on Nick and Daniel either. Nick slammed into the guard who'd tortured him, while Daniel took on the guard who could toss air around.

Within seconds both guards were unconscious on the floor of the van.

I stared at Nick and Daniel, my breathing ragged.

The van slammed to a halt and I heard doors opening. Nick and Daniel readied themselves, fists clenched as they faced the rear door of the van.

As soon as it opened they launched themselves forward, giving the guards no time to use whatever ability they possessed against them. I watched on in satisfaction as the fit young men pummelled the out of shape guards. That'd teach them to rely on their psychic abilities to solve problems for them.

Within minutes all four guards were lying on the side of the road.

We left them there, the three of us piling into the front of the van. It was a tight squeeze, stuck in the middle between Nick and Daniel, but none of us suggested that anyone rode in the back. Like me, I guessed they needed to see where we were going, to face any further threat head on.

Nick was in the driver's seat and he looked past me to

Daniel. 'You ready for this?'

'Hell yeah. Let's go get my sister back.'

'Liam, too,' I said, 'and Rose.'

They both nodded, and Nick started the van, turning it around to face the way we'd come. But when we'd driven a short way we found a new obstacle in our path. The gate to the compound was locked, and a search of the van revealed nothing we could use to open it.

'We could ram our way in,' said Daniel.

'Let's do it,' said Nick.

He backed up the van, no doubt wanting to gain room to get some speed up before ramming the gate. There were only two seatbelts, so Daniel stretched his out as far as it would go to clip the both of us in. I ignored the uncomfortable intimacy of being pressed so close to a stranger. This was no time to be worried about things like that.

Nick gunned the engine, and the van surged forward.

A flash of lightning came from beside the van, and the engine cut off with a whine. The van rolled to a stop.

'Damn it. Now what are we going to do?' Nick thumped the steering wheel.

I turned to Daniel, who was looking out the passenger window. A young woman with flame coloured hair stood beside the road. Daniel yelled for me to unbuckle the seat belt. My fingers fumbled, but I eventually got it done.

Daniel opened the door and jumped out of the car. He ran over to the woman and wrapped his arms around her.

I got out of the van more slowly, conscious of Nick getting out on the driver's side and coming around the front to join us.

'Celeste, we have to get back in there,' said Nick, pointing at the gate. 'Andie's in trouble.'

Celeste grimaced. 'Sorry, I thought you were some of the

81

bad guys. I wouldn't have killed the engine if I'd known you were going to ram the gate.'

Killed the engine? That flash of lightning must have come from her.

'Can you fry the gate controls?' Nick asked, running his hands through his dark hair. His body was tense, eyes worried.

I didn't blame him for being concerned about Andie. I was similarly worried about what was happening to Liam, and Rose. We had to free them. But the gate in front of us was big and strong looking. I didn't see how frying it would do any good.

Unless…

I stepped closer to the gate, looking to see how it opened, hoping it was an electronic keypad or something else Celeste could fry.

But before I could check it out, Celeste gave a cry.

'We need to get out of here,' she said. 'Angel needs my help. They're too strong for her and Ethan to handle on their own.'

Daniel flung up his head, eyes wide. 'Let's go.'

I wanted to protest, to say we couldn't leave until we'd found a way to free Liam and the others, but Daniel and Celeste were on the move. Nick didn't appear to like it any more than I did, but we followed Celeste as she ran for the corner of the compound, leading us back around the side. Halfway there she stumbled, hand going to her head.

A second later she dropped to the ground and didn't move.

Daniel gave an agonised cry as he kneeled beside Celeste, cradling her face in his hands as he pleaded for her to wake up, all to no avail.

What the hell was going on? Were we under attack?

Head swivelling from side to side, I tried to spot whoever had taken Celeste down.

'It's okay,' called out a new voice. It was male; one I did not recognise.

I looked up to see a young man running toward us, a girl who looked exactly like Andie a few steps behind him. He sped to Daniel's side and then kneeled down to place his hands on Celeste's head.

A moment later her eyes flickered, and she opened them to stare up at Daniel. He clasped her in his arms, pulling her upright, and she buried her head into his shoulder.

'Ethan, what was wrong with her?' Nick asked.

'She exhausted herself trying to free you guys,' Ethan said. 'Same as Angel did.' He stood and wrapped an arm around Andie's twin sister.

Angel gave Nick a pat on the arm and then used sign language to tell him something. His shoulders sagged for a moment, and then he straightened. 'We are going to get her out of there. I won't leave without her.'

'Or Liam,' I said, sure I had the gist of the mostly silent conversation.

Ethan and Angel turned to look at me when I spoke. Angel signed something.

'This is Grace,' said Nick. 'Grace, this is Angel, Ethan and Celeste.' He pointed at each of them in turn.

'You're Belinda's cousin,' said Ethan. 'She told us you were missing, but we didn't realise you were here until Andie called out to Angel after she and the others were kidnapped.'

I looked at Angel. 'Is Andie okay? And Liam and Rose?'

Angel's expression darkened.

Ethan held her tighter. 'Angel hasn't been able to contact her since soon after we got here. She's either unconscious or—'

83

Angel pulled herself out of his arms and faced him, shaking her head.

He held up his hands. 'I wasn't going to say dead. I was going to say she could be drugged. That's what stopped you from contacting her when Dr Wood had you.'

The fire in Angel's eyes subsided.

'What about Liam?' I asked. 'He has an ability. You should be able to contact him if he isn't unconscious.'

Ethan shook his head. 'None of us knows the guy. We would never be able to pick out his mental voice in that crowd. There are over a hundred people in there.' He waved a hand at the wall beside us.

'We have to get them out. We can't leave them in there,' I said.

'We will,' said Ethan. 'We just need to wait for reinforcements. Belinda is back at Easton, trying to get in touch with Scott. He's on some top-secret mission for his taskforce and the standard police won't tell her where he is or come out here to help us.'

'That's crazy. I was kidnapped. Same as these guys.' I pointed to Nick and Daniel. 'The police have to do something.'

Celeste's expression soured. 'This isn't the first time the police have ignored what's been going on right under their noses in Easton.'

She was right. The detective assigned to investigate when Belinda had started having visions, Detective Johnson, had been difficult to work with, accusing her of trying to make bad things happen. If it hadn't been for Scott, risking his career to help her, she might never have escaped Dr Frankel's clutches.

'I'm really regretting turning down Scott's offer to join the taskforce,' said Ethan. 'If I hadn't, I'd probably be on the

84

mission with him, and be able to communicate with Angel.'

'What's done is done. We have to deal with what we do have, which is us.' Nick waved a hand around our small group. 'Three people with abilities and three without.'

I shook my head. 'It's not enough. Mark is telekinetic, and so were some of the others in there. They have people who can control fire, and others who can shape water, not to mention guys who can make you see things that aren't there,' I said, remembering what had happened in the back of the van. 'And I have no clue what the rest of them can do.'

'Grace is right. We need back-up. We need Scott and the taskforce to have any chance of freeing Andie and the others,' said Daniel.

It was hard to walk away, not knowing what was happening inside the compound. But I did it, trudging along behind the others as they retreated to where they had stashed two cars. I hopped in the car with Daniel and Celeste, while Nick travelled with Ethan and Angel.

While Daniel drove, I went over scenarios in my head, but couldn't come up with anything that wouldn't get the rest of us captured or killed. Mark was ruthless. He'd ordered Nick, Daniel and me to be disposed of once.

I knew he wouldn't hesitate to do so again if he found out we were still alive.

11

Daniel pulled up in the driveway of a house I had never been to before, but that didn't matter. What did matter was seeing Belinda come flying out of the front door. I jumped out of the car and ran to meet her. We hugged, both of us with tears streaming down our faces.

'I knew you'd be okay. I knew they'd find you,' she said, giving a teary smile.

Her smile wavered when she looked around the group of us. 'Where's Andie?'

'She's still back there,' I said. 'With Liam Devine.'

Her eyes went wide. 'My vision came true?'

I nodded. 'Purple robes and all,' I said, remembering the ceremony where Liam and I had been fake married. I still wore the ring on my finger and I stepped back from Belinda, wondering how I was going to tell her that part without blushing.

Before I had a chance to say anything Daniel ushered us inside, and soon we were all seated around a large dining table, cups of coffee in our hands and a plate of sandwiches to share.

'Andie wasn't able to give us much information about what was going on in that place before Angel lost contact with her,' said Celeste, 'Grace, are you able to fill us in on the rest?'

I took a deep breath and summarised what Mark had told me, leaving out the part about the wedding and his breeding program. I'd save that until Belinda and I were alone.

'Basically,' I said, 'he thinks people with abilities should be in charge of the country and plans on taking Liam to all the major towns and cities. He'll set up dozens of public appearances and get Liam to compel anyone who attends, and who doesn't have an ability, to obey him. That will give him an army of followers who'll do whatever he wants them to do without question or hesitation.'

'I can't believe Liam Devine would do something like that,' said Nick. 'I mean, sure, plenty of celebrities want to live in the limelight, but the guy turned into a recluse after he filmed *God Unleashed*. Not exactly the actions of someone who wants to rule the world.'

I shook my head. 'Liam doesn't want anything to do with Mark's plan. It's Mark who will be in charge. Liam will just be the figurehead, a way to suck enough people in to attend his appearances. Once he has a big enough army, Mark would stage a coup to take over the government.'

'We can't let that happen,' said Ethan.

'But how are we going to stop him?' I asked. 'There's no telling what abilities his followers have. Some of them might not be as strong as you guys, but they outnumber you about fifty to one.'

'I don't know how we're going to do it,' he said. 'But we aren't going to give up until we find a way. This Mark guy has to be stopped.'

'First we need to come up with a plan to get Andie, Liam and Rose out of there,' said Celeste. 'With Andie's help, we become even stronger.' She explained how Andie was a reservoir of power that she and the others could tap into.

'Are you sure you don't have an ability, Grace?' Ethan asked. 'You said Liam couldn't compel you, like he did Nick and Daniel.'

'I swear, I have no ability whatsoever.'

Ethan frowned. 'It could just be dormant, though. Like Belinda's and my abilities. Celeste's too. Only Angel has had hers since she was born. And you said it yourself, that whatever illusion the guards did on Nick and Daniel didn't seem to work on you either.'

Angel signed something, and Ethan gave a nod. 'Angel wants to test you, if that's okay?'

I said yes, though worried about what kind of test she wanted to do. She indicated for me to join her in the space between the dining room and the kitchen. I stood and walked over to her. She took both my hands in hers and closed her eyes. Not sure what I was supposed to be doing, I closed my eyes as well.

Sometime later she released my hands and I opened my eyes. Angel had her head cocked to the side as she gazed at me. Then she turned to Ethan, obviously using telepathy to communicate with him.

He got up and joined us. 'Angel has asked me to see if I can heal you,' he said, pointing to the bruising around my jaw from where I had been punched.

'Sure.'

Ethan gently placed his hands on either side of my head. I once again closed my eyes. I felt a tingle in my skin under his hands, and then a warmth that travelled from my head through to the rest of my body. He dropped his hands and I opened my eyes.

He smiled at me. 'How does that feel?'

I moved my jaw. The pain was gone, along with all the aches I'd gained when Mark first kidnapped me.

'I feel great,' I said. 'What did you do to me?'

'I healed you. It's what I do, when I'm not creating earthquakes,' he said with a shrug.

We sat back down and all of us turned to Angel.

'So,' I said, 'what's the verdict?'

With Celeste translating, Angel said, 'You appear to be immune to mental manipulation. That's why you couldn't see the illusions or be compelled by Liam. But physical abilities affect you, like being tossed around by telekinesis or healed by Ethan.'

'Neither of us could sense you, either,' said Ethan, tapping the side of his head. 'Usually we can sense the presence of others, whether they have an ability or not. But when I close my eyes, it's as though you're not there.'

Belinda's eyes went wide. 'Ethan's right. It's as if you're invisible. I never realised before now, that I don't sense when you are close. I could see you in the vision though, so your immunity obviously doesn't have any effect on that aspect of my abilities.'

'Immunity, huh?' I sat back, running it through my head. 'So that probably means I'm not harbouring some latent ability that is just waiting for the right trigger to awaken?'

'It looks that way,' said Ethan.

'Hm.' I wasn't sure how I felt about that. It might have been nice to suddenly gain the power to throw people with just a wave of my hand, to get Mark back for all the pain he had caused me. Then again, I had seen how much pain visions of bad things caused Belinda. It had also made her, and the others, targets for unscrupulous scientists. Maybe being immune was a good thing.

But knowing I was immune to mental manipulation was one thing. We still needed to figure out how to free Liam, Andie and Rose. After an hour of brainstorming, no one had any ideas beyond waiting for Scott to contact Belinda, so we could marshal the taskforce onto the job.

By then it was getting late. I called my parents to reassure them I was fine, only to discover Mark had covered his tracks well. He'd been right when he said I wouldn't be missed. He'd had someone pretend to be me, who called my parents and my boss to say I needed to get away for a while. I guess, if he had people who could create illusions for him then having someone convince my Mum and Dad that I was talking to them on the phone would be easy.

He hadn't tried that on Belinda though, no doubt aware she'd see through the ruse. She said Mum and Dad told her I was on retreat, but she'd never believed it. She'd had a horrible feeling from the moment she woke up Saturday morning, even before she got out of bed and found I'd disappeared from the flat. That was what led her to going to Angel and the others for help to find me, when all her visions gave her was the same image of me standing beside Liam in our purple robes.

After it was decided we should spend the night, Belinda and I got comfortable beside each other in a double bed in a guest bedroom. But even though I was mentally exhausted, whatever Ethan had done to heal my body meant I was wide awake.

'Care to share what's on your mind?' said Belinda, on her side and facing me.

In a quiet voice, I told her everything I'd left out earlier, glad the light was off so she wouldn't see my blush when I described the moment Liam had kissed me in front of Mark and his followers.

'He did it to make Mark think we were going along with his plan,' I said.

'I'm pretty sure he could have done that without putting his tongue in your mouth,' she said in a wry tone. 'Guys do not kiss girls like that, whatever the motivation, unless they like them. Believe me, getting caught up in a stressful situation can lead to you falling for someone in record time.

90

Look at me and Scott.'

She was right. Their relationship had blossomed in the time since they first met during the investigation into her visions and her subsequent kidnapping by Dr Frankel. From the sound of it, Daniel and Celeste had also got together during a bad situation. The same with Nick and Andie, and Angel and Ethan.

Warmth flared through me at the thought of continuing a relationship with Liam once we got him and the others away from the compound.

I was sure Mark wouldn't do anything drastic to him, to punish him for not obeying his orders. He needed Liam to fulfil his plan. But what about Andie and Rose?

Worry for Liam and the others kept me awake long into the night. When I did manage to fall asleep, it felt as if I'd just closed my eyes when Belinda cried out, her hand lashing around and hitting me in the face.

I sat up and nudged her shoulder, brushing hair back from her face as she opened her eyes and looked at me, eyes wide with horror.

'It's okay,' I said. 'It was just a nightmare.'

'It wasn't a nightmare,' she said, voice shaking. 'It was a vision. Liam is going to die.'

My heart seemed to stop beating. Then it started again in a rush as I jumped out of bed and ran for the door, yelling for Angel and the others.

They came running from their respective rooms, alarm in their eyes.

'Belinda had a vision,' I said, words tumbling over each other. 'She said Liam is going to die. We have to stop it from happening.'

Celeste hurried over to me, grasping my shoulders. 'Grace, it's okay. We'll help. Just calm down.' She looked

91

over my shoulder. 'Belinda, what exactly did you see?'

'A man in a white outfit stood on a stage. Andie and a young woman with curly hair were there with him. They were both wearing white dresses like the one Grace is wearing and were kneeling in front of him. Liam was off to the side. Two big guys who were also in white were holding his arms. The main guy was walking backward and forward in front of Andie and the other girl, saying something about how they couldn't be trusted and were working against the good of the Order. He sentenced them to death. He waved his hand and they both grabbed their throats. It looked as if he was strangling them using telekinesis.'

I gulped in air, rubbing my throat at the memory of being strangled just the way she described.

Belinda threw an anguished glance my way and then continued talking. 'Liam pulled away from the men holding him and ran over, punching the telekinetic guy. The man swung around and suddenly Liam was flying backward off the stage. He landed on the ground, hard, his head at an odd angle. People were screaming, and I could tell he was dead. I'm so sorry, Grace.'

I shook my head, straightening my shoulders. 'There's no need to be sorry. We're going to stop it from happening.'

'What about Andie? Was she okay?' Nick moved forward and grasped Belinda by the shoulders. 'Tell me she's going to be okay.'

'I think so. It seemed when Liam attacked him whatever control he had over the girls broke. They were rubbing their throats, but they were still alive when the vision cut out.'

'That doesn't mean Mark won't try again,' I said, pushing aside my fear for Liam to focus on what had to be done. 'His entire plan hinged on using Liam's ability to compel people to obey him. Without him, he won't be able to take control of the country. He'll be furious. He could take it out on Andie and Rose.'

'Grace is right,' said Ethan. 'We have to get out there and stop Mark.'

'But we still haven't heard from Scott. We'll be on our own,' said Celeste.

'Hey, you and Angel didn't give up when Dr Wood held you prisoner. You even managed to knock some sense into my head,' said Ethan. 'We can't let Liam die. Or Andie and this girl Rose. We have to stop Belinda's vision from coming true.'

'How long do we have?' Daniel asked.

'It was daylight,' said Belinda. 'The sun was shining through the windows, but it wasn't at its full strength, so I would say it is going to happen early morning.'

I looked out the window of the lounge room. The sky was just starting to lighten. 'We don't have much time. It takes at least an hour to drive out there. We need to hurry. We can come up with a plan on the way.'

There was no time for further discussion. Within minutes Nick and Daniel were once again dressed in the white outfits they'd escaped in. I'd slept in my dress, so didn't need to change, but the others found white clothes to help them blend in. I gratefully accepted the hair tie Celeste offered me, quickly braiding my hair back like hers.

We again piled into two cars. We would need the extra seats for Liam, Andie and Rose on the return trip. I refused to let doubt that we were going to save them enter my head.

We would be in time.

We would find a way to stop Mark from killing Liam.

12

Daniel drove, with Celeste in the front beside him, while Belinda and I shared the backseat. Nick was in the car behind us, driving Angel and Ethan. With two people in each vehicle capable of communicating telepathically, we scraped together a plan.

Ethan would create an earthquake under the compound, while Celeste used her ability to call lightning to further distract the members of the Order. Meanwhile, Angel would tackle the lock on the rear gate, and be ready to hurl a fireball at anyone who tried to stop us.

Nick, Daniel and I were to provide back-up to the ones with an ability, to use more mundane methods to distract and disarm them as best we could. Belinda had an ability, but I didn't see how visions of bad things happening would be of much help. We already knew something bad was going to happen if we didn't stop Mark in time.

'It's not just visions,' said Belinda, a squeamish expression on her face. 'I can get inside someone's head, make them see and do what I want them to do. But I have to really concentrate and would only be able to do one person at a time.'

I held her hand as she explained how she had convinced Dr Frankel to untie her by making him see himself doing that, and how he had been rendered unconscious as soon as she stopped what she was doing. She'd been through so much, and I hadn't known half of it.

'You should've told me,' I said, giving her hand a

squeeze.

She gave me a sheepish smile. 'I didn't want you to think I was some kind of freak. I was worried it would make you feel uncomfortable with what I could do.'

'Really?' I raised my eyebrows. 'We've been friends our entire lives. Nothing you could do would make me uncomfortable.' I let a smile curl my lips. 'Except for that make-out session you were having with Scott last week. Walking in on one of those was more than enough for me.'

She shook her head, a sly grin on her face as she leaned in close and said in a low voice, 'Just as long as I don't have to sit and watch you and Liam make-out instead.'

I could feel the heat swamping my cheeks and I glanced toward the front seats to see if Daniel and Celeste had overheard what she'd said. I should never have told her about the fake wedding and our first kiss as husband and wife.

'Knocking people unconscious sounds like a good idea, especially if they are using their abilities against us,' said Daniel, turning to look at us. His features were pulled tight, no doubt worried about what was happening to Andie.

A hard knot of anxiety formed in my stomach at the thought we might arrive too late. The sun was fully up now, and Belinda had said it was early morning in her vision. We had to make it.

I leaned forward, tapping Daniel on the shoulder. 'Drive faster.'

'I'm going as fast as I safely can,' he said, not taking his eyes off the road.

Minutes later we turned a corner and I caught sight of a large wall blocking the roadway. Daniel pulled his car off to the side of the road a couple of hundred metres back. I hoped it was far enough away that our vehicles wouldn't get caught up in the earthquake Ethan was going to make.

We got out of the car and ran for the gate, with Angel and the others right behind us. At the gate we stopped for a moment to ready ourselves.

Last time Angel and the others had rushed in, letting Mark know they were there somehow. This time Angel, Celeste and Ethan stood with eyes closed and heads turned in all different directions. It had to be some mental thing they used to determine whether the way forward was clear or not.

When they opened their eyes, and all three of them gave a nod, we silently set off for the road at the back of the compound. The van we'd driven back here was no longer sitting in the middle of the roadway. I hoped all the guards' attention was focused on the front gate Angel said had already been repaired.

Angel and Celeste stood side by side to determine what kind of locking mechanism the gate had and if they could unlock it. A soft click came, and it swung outwards. Daniel caught it with his hand, not letting it swing too far, but just enough for the seven of us to slip through. He picked a stick up off the ground and placed it between the gate and the jamb to keep it from locking us in.

'In case we need to leave in a hurry,' he said quietly.

I gave a nod, hoping when we did use the gate to escape, Liam and the others would be with us.

We hurried through the compound, past the shed and dam, without encountering anyone. The place was eerily silent as we weaved our way through the demountable buildings and drew near the church.

'They're all in that building over there,' said Ethan, a look of concentration on his face as he pointed at the church. 'There's so much talking going on, it's like a constant buzz in my head.'

I cocked my head, still unable to hear anything. Then it

clicked. He meant mental talking. It was like the time Mark presented Liam and me to his followers. No one spoke vocally.

I pointed at the back of the church. 'That's where we were held,' I said. 'But there are no windows. Do any of you have the power to break through walls?' If one of them could cut a hole in the wall to our room, we'd be able to get Liam, Rose and Andie out without having to go through the people congregating in the main part of the church.

'It wouldn't work,' said Celeste. 'Angel scanned those rooms and they're empty. Everyone is in the first part, including Andie and your friends.'

If they were inside the main part of the church, then they had to be on the stage.

Mark was getting ready to execute Rose and Andie, and Liam was about to die trying to save them.

I urged the others forward, jaw clenched to stop me from crying out.

We ran for the front door.

It was open. We lined up to the side of it.

Belinda, Angel, Celeste and Ethan stuck their heads around the edges of the doorway one at a time to see the layout. Then the four of them stood facing each other, planning the attack in their heads, somehow able to shield their thoughts so no one inside the church would hear them. We couldn't risk making any noise now we were so close. Daniel, Nick and I had to just stand there. I wondered if they felt as useless as me, without being able to hear what was being said.

Then Angel made a few quick signs, and they nodded. So now it was just me who was out of the loop.

I was really starting to wish I wasn't immune to mental manipulation. I wanted to know what was going on, to be in

97

on the decision making. Not just stand there and wait for someone to tell me what to do or find out after the fact.

But I wasn't psychic.

I would have to suck it up and do my best to stay out of their way and to help where I could. I would focus all my effort on getting to Liam. I had to save him.

After what felt like hours, Angel gave a nod. It was time to move.

I held back a gasp as two fireballs appeared in Angel's hands. A crackle came from beside her before sparks began running over Celeste's fingers. I turned to Ethan to see nothing coming from his hands, but his eyes had changed colour and were now a swirling mix of green, gold and brown.

Daniel and Nick both tensed up as Angel stepped through the doorway.

As she did so, the ground began to rumble far beneath us, and the demountable buildings nearby began to shake. A loud crackle came from the sky a split second before a bolt of lightning speared the ground in front of the construction site on the other side of the clearing, the frame of the half-built buildings shaking.

The hairs on my arms stood on end at this display of power.

The response from inside the large building was almost immediate.

Shouts rose, the mental communication clearly not a match for their shock as they realised they were under attack.

People pushed back to the sides of the room as Angel walked in their midst with her hands blazing. Celeste and Ethan stayed beside the front door to keep a path clear for us and to make sure no one tried to get to us from outside.

It was up to Daniel, Nick, Belinda and me to shadow Angel as she headed for the stage.

Over the heads of the people I saw Liam standing on the right side of the stage, guards on either side of him.

But where were Andie and Rose?

There. In the middle of the stage. Kneeling in front of Mark.

Rose had her head bowed but Andie glared defiantly at the man looming over her. I had to admire her spunk. She was showing no fear as she struggled to her feet.

'It's over,' she said. 'Your little cult or whatever it is you have going on here is finished.'

He sneered back at her. 'Nothing will stop me.' He flung out his hand and she gasped, hands going to her throat. Beside me, Nick gave a roar and barrelled forward, running past Angel and leaping onto the stage.

Mark swung around to meet his charge, and with a wave of his hand Nick was flung backward to land on the floor of the church.

I froze. This was what Belinda had seen happen to Liam, and it killed him.

Was Nick dead?

Andie, freed from Mark's telekinetic grip, launched herself off the stage and knelt at Nick's side. My paralysis broke and I ran toward them, relieved to hear Nick groan as Andie helped him to his feet.

'Grace, look out.'

I turned at Liam's shout, finding at least half a dozen men bearing down on us. One had flames in his hands, smaller than the ones Angel was able to produce but no doubt just as dangerous. I looked around me for a weapon.

On the stage, Liam was struggling with the men holding his arms. He made a massive lurch and one of them let go. Liam instantly swung a fist at the other guy's face. The second guard let go and Liam dodged their attempts to recapture him as he leapt off the stage and ran toward me. He was tackled to the ground when one of his guards launched at him.

'Stay away from her,' Liam said to the men advancing on me, even as he twisted to fight the guard off.

I faced the men, knowing Nick was still too groggy to be any help. He was supported by Andie, who looked around her at the chaos our arrival had precipitated.

Then Belinda was there, standing in front of me, arm out as she faced the man with the flaming hands. He faltered mid-step, eyes clouding over, and one foot suspended in the air as whatever she was doing took hold. The two men directly behind him stiffened, panicked expressions on their faces.

The rest surged around them, jostling them as they went, breaking the spell Belinda had created to hold them in place.

We were going to be overwhelmed at any minute.

Celeste appeared at my side, lightning sparking from her fingertips as she pointed at the men. Their bodies shook as the electrical current surged through them, then they fell on the ground, limbs still twitching.

The ground shook beneath us, dust falling from the ceiling as the timber beams groaned.

Suddenly Daniel was beside me, lunging forward to help Liam with his attacker. One swift punch and the guard dropped to the ground. Liam hurried to my side and wrapped his arms around me.

I hugged him back, lifting my head to tell him how thankful I was he was okay.

His mouth descended, lips claiming mine and I clung to him as his arms tightened around me to the point of being almost painful. But I didn't care. He was alive. We'd saved him.

He lifted his head and I took a deep breath.

We'd saved Liam, but that didn't mean we were safe. We still had to get out of there.

13

I twisted in Liam's arms, not wanting to break contact with him now we'd been reunited, and scanned the church looking for the others. Angel was using fire to fend off a large group of people on the other side of the church. Andie and Nick were beside her, and I presumed Angel was drawing from her sister's reservoir of power to keep up her wall of flame.

Ethan was still near the front door, standing to one side as a crush of people ran outside. Belinda, Celeste and Daniel were with Liam and me. So that left only Rose for me to find.

There were so many people rushing to and fro, all of them dressed in white, it was hard to distinguish individuals. Then I spotted her, and my heart skipped. She was still on the stage, with Mark.

He had hold of her arm as he stood near the edge, his free hand pointed at us as his followers scattered.

'I will not let you get away with this!' His voice was a screech, face twisted into a mask of hate. 'You will not destroy everything I have worked for.'

'It's over, Mark,' said Liam, his voice firm and calm, though I could feel the tension running through his body. 'No one else needs to get hurt.'

'I will bury you all before I see you ruin the Order.'

He lifted his free hand and pointed at the ceiling. The timber beams began to groan even louder than when Ethan had made the ground shake.

'Father, no.' Rose pulled her arm free and stood in front of him. 'Let them go.'

'Silence.' He thrust her aside and she fell to her knees. 'You sided with them. You are not one of us. You're deaf.'

Tears streamed down Rose's face as the words hit home.

'Father, please, I'm begging you. Don't do this.' She scrambled to her feet and moved toward him, clutching at his arm.

He wrenched free and slapped her across the face. 'Traitor. You are no longer my daughter.' He waved his hand and she was flung backward, landing on her back halfway across the stage.

I pulled out of Liam's arms and ran closer to the stage. 'Rose, come with us.'

A loud groan sounded over my head, dust falling as the timber beams shifted once more, and I yelled at her to get up. To get out of there.

All of Mark's attention was fixed on the ceiling, ignoring us for the moment.

Rose slowly got to her feet and limped to the edge of the stage.

There was a deafening crack as the ceiling directly above the stage collapsed, the timber support beams plummeting down and bringing a large chunk of the ceiling with them.

Dust filled the air, choking me, and I shielded my eyes, searching the stage for Rose. I couldn't see her or Mark, only a jagged pile of timber where the stage used to be. I ran toward it, screaming Rose's name. Someone grabbed me around the waist and pulled me back.

'No, we have to get Rose.' I struggled free and ran to where the front of the stage used to be.

More groans and creaks came from what remained of the ceiling.

'Grace, we have to get out of here,' said Liam. 'The whole building is about to fall down.'

Tears drenched my cheeks as I faced him, shaking my head.

Grief filled his eyes, lips clenched tight. He grabbed my hand and gave a tug.

Wordlessly, I let him pull me away. We picked up speed as we ran for the doors, our free hands over our heads in a vain attempt to ward off the ceiling should it collapse.

We burst outside, hand in hand, as a thunderous crash came from behind us, a wave of air sending us tumbling into the clearing in front of the church. Liam's hand was wrenched from mine and I wrapped my arms around my head as I landed heavily, pain coursing through my body and robbing me of breath.

Hands grabbed me under the arms, pulling me back from the building that was now no more than a crumpled pile of broken timber.

Silence reigned as the dust settled, the devastating image plastered into my brain forever. There was no sign of Rose or Mark, nothing to show where they were buried under the rubble or if they had survived the ceiling caving in on them.

Hands grasped my head and warmth flowed through my body.

I turned to see Ethan kneeling beside me, dust and grime covering him from head to toe.

My aches and pains disappeared instantly. Then he let go and moved to where Liam lay on the ground a short distance away. Blood poured from a gash on his temple. His eyes were closed, skin pale. So very pale.

No.

We could not have just gone through all that to lose him now.

I got to my feet and ran to his side as Ethan knelt beside him and took hold of his head.

Breath held, I scanned Liam's body, sagging in relief when I saw the rise and fall of his chest.

He was alive.

As Ethan ministered to him, he gave a soft groan, eyelids fluttering.

'Don't move,' I said, voice choked with tears of relief as I smoothed hair back from his forehead. 'You're going to be okay.'

Ethan leaned back, exhaustion racking his features as he looked over and gave me a nod. Then Angel came and helped him to his feet.

I looked around the clearing in front of the ruined church. There were over a dozen of Mark's followers lying on the ground sporting injuries, but Ethan was clearly in no condition to heal them. Luckily, it didn't look as if any of my friends needed to be healed.

From what I could see, Angel, Celeste and Belinda were just as exhausted as Ethan.

More of the Order's followers moved amongst the injured, matching looks of shock on their faces at what had transpired. None of them paid any attention to us. It appeared Mark's Order of the Arcane was no more.

'Grace?'

I looked down to see that Liam's eyes were open. I smiled at him, leaning forward to kiss him lightly on the lips.

His arms came up to rest on my hips and we stayed like that for a long moment. Then I sat back and helped him to a sitting position. He gazed around the clearing, shaking his head.

Then he looked over at the rubble that had once held our prison cell.

He sighed, sagging against me as we both stared at it.

So much had happened since we'd both been brought to

this place, events that had changed us completely.

As I looked around at the others I knew they felt the same way.

But most of all I felt the loss of Rose. I hadn't even had the chance to get to know her properly. Now she was buried under the ruined church, after doing everything she could to save our lives.

I could only hope that somehow, by a miracle, she was still alive.

'Daniel has called the police. They're sending emergency teams here. If she's alive, they'll find her,' said Andie, coming over to stand beside us.

I gave a bitter laugh. 'They didn't want to know anything about this place when Belinda and the others called to say what was going on. Now, when it's all over, they finally agree to come out here?'

Andie gave a nod. 'It's not fair, I know. But we did everything we could.'

Yes, but it hadn't been enough.

I stared at the bright vests of the rescue workers as they painstakingly worked their way through the rubble. They'd retrieved Mark's body an hour before, but they hadn't found Rose.

Liam stood beside me, his arm wrapped around my waist, but I couldn't bring myself to sink into the comfort he offered.

In the aftermath of the building collapse it'd been utter turmoil, people running every which way to escape falling timbers. We'd managed to get clear, but many others had not been so lucky, and were pinned under the debris.

Within hours the place had been crawling with emergency personnel, treating the wounded and searching for those who were still trapped inside the remains of the building. All of them had been found, many injured but alive except for Mark. Now it was only Rose who was to be recovered.

She was in a pocket somewhere, hidden and maybe unconscious since there had been no cries for help and Angel and the others had been unable to sense her presence.

Maybe she was immune like me, and that's why they couldn't sense her.

But she was there. She had to be.

I wasn't leaving until they found her.

I watched on as the last of the injured were placed in two of the three remaining ambulances. The doors closed on their patients and they moved slowly through the gaps between the demountable buildings, heading for the Easton Base Hospital. One ambulance remained, waiting for Rose.

As the day wore on, the looks on the faces of the emergency workers became more dejected. Volunteers offered us food and drinks, but though Liam urged me to eat, I couldn't choke anything down. My throat grew increasingly tight as the hours passed with no sign of Rose.

I clutched the fresh cup of coffee a worker had foisted on me, feeling the polystyrene crack under the pressure I was applying to it, the hot liquid stinging my fingers. I ignored the pain, gaze focused on the rubble as a newly arrived search and rescue dog worked its way over broken beams.

The dog scented a section of the rubble near where the stage had been and began to bark, remaining in place.

I dropped my coffee, feeling a hot splatter on my legs as I surged forward.

Rescue workers scrambled to get to the area the dog had indicated, and I didn't take my eyes off them as they carefully shifted the rubble.

'She's here,' one of them called out.

Thankful tears flooded my eyes and I let Liam wrap me in

his arms, burrowing into his embrace, still not willing to take my eyes off the rescue effort until I knew Rose was going to be okay.

It felt like an eternity before they began the painstaking process of transferring Rose to a stretcher and carried her off the rubble.

Two paramedics were waiting at the edge, and they immediately set to work assessing their patient, expressions grave.

'She's not breathing,' said the female paramedic. 'I'm not getting a pulse.'

I shook my head, pulling away from Liam and looking for Ethan. He was already in motion, moving toward the paramedics. He knelt beside them and placed his hands on Rose's head.

'What do you think you're doing?' the male paramedic asked.

Ethan ignored him, focusing all his attention on Rose.

I held my breath as he worked on her. Had his power regenerated enough to enable him to heal her?

Rose gave a cough, eyes fluttering open, and I sagged back against Liam.

'What the hell?' The male paramedic looked from Rose to Ethan. 'How did you do that?'

Shoulders sagging, Ethan got to his feet. Angel rushed forward to wrap an arm around his waist.

'Ryan, focus,' said the female paramedic to her partner.

He turned his attention to Rose once more and within minutes she was in the back of the ambulance, on her way to hospital.

'She'll be okay, Grace. I got to her in time,' said Ethan, his exhaustion coming out in his voice.

'Thank you,' I said, leaning over and kissing him on the

cheek.

Tears in my eyes, I looked over at all of my new friends. None of them had made any effort to leave. If it wasn't for their help, none of this would've been possible. Liam would be dead, and who knows how many more would've paid the ultimate price to fulfil Mark's plans for the Order of the Arcane.

The Order was no more.

I turned to Liam and gave him a teary smile. 'Let's go home.'

Liam snaked his arm around my waist. 'Sounds good.'

We started walking for the gate, keeping out of the way of the rescue workers as they continued to process the site.

'You will stay, won't you?' I asked, looking up at Liam. 'In Easton, I mean. You're not thinking of turning into a recluse again?'

'Of course I'm staying; I still owe you a dinner. Besides, why would I want to go back to my beach shack when everything I want is right here?' He gave me a squeeze. 'I will have to check in with the family though, let them know I'm okay, in case any of this turns up on the news.' He waved a hand behind us. 'It's been a while since I visited them.'

He stopped walking and turned me to face him. 'Will you come with me, to meet my parents?'

Pleasure had me beaming. 'Sure, I will, after you meet mine.'

His smile dimmed somewhat, and then he shrugged. 'After everything else that has happened lately, meeting your parents should be a piece of cake.'

I laughed along with him, sure everything was going to be perfect from now on.

But that feeling soon faded when we reached the area where Ethan and Daniel had left their cars and found three ambulances parked haphazardly near them, their rear doors wide open.

Six paramedics, amongst them the two who'd tended to Rose, lay on the ground nearby. None of them moved.

Ethan ran toward the paramedics.

'They're alive,' he called out. 'I think they've been drugged.'

I ran to the nearest ambulance, seeing the empty bed in the back. I quickly checked the other two ambulances, finding them also empty.

Where were the patients?

Where was Rose?

I spun in a circle, scanning the nearby bushland.

'They're not here,' said Celeste, moving to my side and placing a hand on my arm. 'There's no one here but us.'

'Are you sure? Check again.' I clutched her arm.

'We've all checked, Grace.' She waved a hand over to where Ethan and the others stood looking down on the paramedics. 'None of us can sense anyone else except for the rescue workers back at the Order's compound.'

It didn't make sense.

Rose was barely conscious. The patients that had been in the other two ambulances were also in no fit state to pull a disappearing act.

We'd just got Rose back. We couldn't lose her again.

Nick had his phone out and within minutes the search and rescue dog was sniffing around the ambulances as rescue workers took care of the drugged paramedics. But this time the dog didn't bark, seeming to find no trace of Rose or the other missing patients.

'They must have been taken away in other vehicles,' said Liam, pointing to what looked like fresh tyre tracks leading from the ambulance Rose had been in.

'But who would take them?' I asked.

'I don't know. But we'll find her. We won't give up,' he said.

'None of us will,' said Andie.

I looked behind me to see her and the others, all of them with matching expressions of worry and determination on their faces.

'No matter what it takes, we will find Rose,' said Liam, bringing my attention back to him.

I allowed him to take me in his arms once more, resting my head against his chest and listening to his heartbeat.

He was right.

No matter what it took, we would find her together.

Book Six

Spirit Unleashed

1

A heavy weight sat on my chest, pinning me down. I struggled to draw in air, dust coating my mouth and nose.

'Rose.'

The voice sounded distant, muffled, making it impossible for me to make out who was calling my name.

I tried to turn my head, to see if I could spot anyone, but couldn't move. Something was wedged on either side of me, as well as on top of me, keeping me immobile.

A low groan came from nearby, and I shivered at the agony encased in the sound. The groan came again, followed by dull thuds and the sound of more muffled voices. I felt something shift on my right, loosening the pressure on the side of my head, and I was now able to turn that way, searching for whoever was groaning.

At first I couldn't make sense of what I saw. It was a dusty maze of broken timber and plaster. Pinpricks of light wove their way through the debris, creating a sea of shadows.

I gasped, memory kicking in.

Father had used his ability to bring part of the church roof down, trying to kill Liam and Grace, furious with them for interfering with his plans to execute Andie and me.

The weight on my chest felt light compared to the knowledge Father had wanted me dead, blaming me for the disappearance of the four men he'd ordered to dispose of Grace, Daniel and Nick, and another two men who had disappeared the day before that. He'd called me a traitor, accused me of being behind everything that had gone wrong since he put into action his plan to set Liam and Grace up as divine figureheads for the Order of the Arcane.

Nothing I'd said could convince him of my innocence, his fury hammering into me. I'd been kneeling on the stage, Andie at my side, sure I was going to die, when Grace and the others had stormed into the church to rescue us.

Were they alive? Were they trapped somewhere under the rubble with me?

As my eyes adjusted to the gloom, I glimpsed something white. A leg encased in white pants. Someone was buried under a pile of timber near me. I squinted, trying to see who it was, following the flashes of clothing to map their position.

Bile rose in my throat when I looked into my father's unseeing eyes. Blood and dust covered his face but I knew it was him. Just as I knew he was dead. Relief swamped me, swiftly followed by guilt. Despite everything, he was my father. I shouldn't be glad he was dead. I may have wanted to leave the Order, to run away with Grace and the others, but this was not how I wanted to gain my freedom.

Not that being trapped under part of the church meant I was free.

But if Father hadn't been the one groaning, then someone else must be trapped nearby.

I pulled my eyes away from Father's lifeless body and opened my mouth to call out to whoever was trapped with me, to let them know they weren't alone. But there was another shift in the rubble above me, more dust raining down and into my open mouth, choking me.

The weight on my chest increased, and it became harder to breathe. Coughing up dust, lungs screaming for air, I fought to move.

It was useless.

My entire body was pinned down. I registered the

increase in light on the other side of Father's body and the distant voices became clearer. Rescuers, combing the rubble for survivors. I just had to hold on long enough for them to find me.

I lapsed in and out of consciousness, waiting to be rescued. After some time, no idea how long, I looked over and saw that Father's body was gone, even more light streaming through gaps in the rubble.

It hurt to breathe, throat dry and abraded, pain washing through me each time I sucked in air. My breaths were getting shallower, the moments of unconsciousness seemingly longer. The weight on my chest was so heavy now my body had gone numb beneath it. I was cold, tired, barely able to make the effort to keep breathing. I had to let go. Couldn't hold on any longer.

I closed my eyes, sure I would never open them again, taking one last breath.

A wave of energy washed over me. It felt as if I was in the middle of a whirlpool. My body spun every which way. Silvery light exploded around me, penetrating my closed eyelids. Then came a snap, my body lurched, and I felt myself rising.

Was I being rescued?

I opened my eyes and found myself hovering above the ruins of what had once been the church for the Order of the Arcane, jagged timber jutting up out of the pile as rescue workers in bright vests worked their way over it.

The church had been demolished, no part of it left intact.

How could anyone have survived that?

How could I be above it?

I looked down at my body, and a shiver swept over me. I was bathed in silver, my form indistinct, diaphanous, the way I would expect a ghost to appear.

Was I dead?

I looked around, and spotted several ambulances and police cars, people milling around the clearing in front of the ruined church. My gaze settled on Grace, cradled in Liam's arms. Tears flowed unchecked down her cheeks as she watched the rescue workers pick their way through the rubble.

Was this a dream? A vision?

What was happening to me?

A small black dog roamed over the rubble. As I watched on, the dog sat down and began to bark. Moments later rescue workers were swarming over the area where the dog had been. Four of them lifted a thick timber beam and one of them gave a shout.

'She's here,' he called out.

Grace pulled out of Liam's arms and ran toward the rubble. Liam joined her, and they stood side by side, never taking their eyes off the rescuers as they worked to free a body from the rubble and place them on a stretcher.

The person they found was female, the white dress she wore covered in dust, curly brown hair greyed with it. I moved closer, looking at the pale face of the young woman being carried over to a waiting ambulance.

It was me.

My physical body.

A thin silver cord, as diaphanous as my ghostly form, connected me to it. Still struggling to understand what had happened, and reeling with the possibility I was dead, I floated closer.

One of the paramedics leaned over my body, and I felt my ghost form ripple when she attached something to my chest. Yet my physical body remained still.

The paramedic removed the device and shook her head as she looked at her partner. 'She's not breathing. I'm not getting

118

a pulse.'

A young man with black hair and green eyes ran over and placed his hands on my head, while Grace watched with fresh tears streaming down her cheeks, hand covering her mouth.

'What do you think you're doing?' the male paramedic asked.

Another ripple went through me, only this one was so much stronger than before. It whirled me around in the air, and then a sharp tug pulled me closer to my body.

I slammed into it, a cough forcing its way out of my lungs.

I opened my eyes, blinking up at the young man as he backed away.

'What the hell? How did you do that?' the male paramedic asked him.

'Ryan, focus,' said the female paramedic.

They both leaned over me, blocking my view, and the stretcher I was on was pushed into the back of the ambulance. I was dimly aware of straps being placed around me, securing me to the stretcher, and monitors attached to my body.

'It's okay, Rose. You're going to be okay,' said the paramedic as she slipped an oxygen mask over my face.

I allowed my eyes to close, feeling the rumble of the engine before the ambulance began to move.

Sometime later I felt it come to a stop and forced my eyes open. We must be at the hospital.

'Why are we stopped?' the paramedic beside me called out.

Before her partner could reply the back door of the ambulance opened.

'Who are you?' The paramedic's voice was high pitched, alarmed.

I heard a thud and a cry of pain, and then a man dressed in

119

a black uniform, a mask covering his face, unstrapped me and lifted me off the bed.

I struggled, trying to get out of his arms, but I was too weak, my struggles ineffectual as he pulled off the oxygen mask and handed me over to someone waiting outside the ambulance. Something was placed over my head, made of a thick black cloth, and my breathing sounded raspy in my ears as I was carried away.

I was laid down on a soft surface similar to the stretcher I had just been on. More straps were placed over me, and I heard muffled voices before a door slammed shut. I heard an engine start, and then came the sensation of movement.

It was hard to breathe with the cloth over my face, but I managed to suck in enough air to keep me from suffocating. Dizziness swamped me, making it hard to think, to make sense of what had happened.

Who would kidnap me from the back of an ambulance?

Whatever the young man with black hair had done to heal me had made a huge difference, but I must still need medical treatment, or I wouldn't have been in an ambulance in the first place. I also wouldn't feel so weak if I had been healed completely.

So many questions ran through my head, but I had no answers for any of them.

After what seemed like forever I felt the vehicle slowing down. It came to a stop, the engine still running, and I heard voices outside. Then the vehicle started moving again.

A short time later the vehicle came to a complete stop, the engine cutting off, and I heard a door opening. The stretcher I was on was rolled out of the van and I turned my head, trying to see something through the cloth to explain what was happening to me.

I saw faint pricks of light, but nothing else.

I heard more voices, but with my head still muffled it was hard to work out what they were saying.

I only managed to catch a word here or there.

'Treatment room...'

'Level One...'

I was moved again, hearing more doors open and close before the straps holding me down were undone. Hands lifted me, and I was transferred to another surface. I spread out my hands and found a hard mattress with a stiff sheet over top.

Was this a hospital after all?

More straps were placed over me and then the hood was removed.

I blinked against the sudden brightness as a light beamed down on me. Squinting, I looked around the room I was in to see another bed beside me, with some kind of medical equipment resting on a small trolley next to it.

The other bed was empty.

'Out of my way,' said a brisk voice.

I turned to see a man with thick glasses and a bushy beard pushing between two men in black uniforms. He stepped to the side of the bed I was on and peered down at me. I opened my mouth, to ask him where I was and what was going on, but my throat was so dry, tongue sticky, all that came out was a croak.

He ignored my attempt to communicate as he gazed at me. 'Oh, yes, she will do nicely.'

He waved to someone behind him. 'I want full updates on her condition and a report as to when you can begin testing in one hour.'

He moved away and a woman in a white lab coat, dark brown hair slicked back into a severe bun, took his place. Her attractive features were fixed in a scowl as she ran her hands efficiently over my body, using a range of medical

121

instruments to assess my health.

I again tried to ask what was going on. She had to be a doctor, but why steal me from the ambulance and bring me here?

It had to be a hospital, right? But what kind of testing had the man with the beard meant?

It was all too much, everything that had happened since Father brought Grace and Liam to the compound.

I couldn't think, couldn't pull in enough air to ease the ache in my chest.

Tears trickled down my cheeks as I lay there.

A long time later the doctor stopped poking and prodding me and stepped back. I gathered my energy and turned my head to watch her as she scribbled something down on the clipboard now clasped in her hands.

'Send him in,' she said to one of the men in the black uniforms. He strode to the door and left the room. Moments later he returned with a man dressed in jeans and a shirt.

I recognised him as Anthony. He was one of Father's men, one of two who had disappeared a couple of days ago on a routine supply run.

'Well, what can she do?' The doctor pointed at me.

He screwed up his mouth. 'That's Rose, Davidson's daughter. She's useless. Never manifested any abilities.'

Her scowl deepened as she gazed at me. 'His daughter?'

I cringed back, scared by the cruel light that appeared in her eyes as she reached out a hand. She clutched my shoulder and dug her fingers in, making me wince.

'You're sure she doesn't have an ability?'

'Yeah, he used to complain about it all the time, how she was deaf and wouldn't be able to carry on his legacy.'

The doctor let go of my shoulder as fresh tears stung my eyes. Not because of the pain she'd caused, but the sting of his words. Father had thought I was useless. I'd known it, but to hear someone else say it made me feel worse.

The doctor shook her head and moved back from the bed. 'At this rate, Dr Frankel's clients are going to be extremely disappointed. None of the new people you dragged in here have much ability at all, and this one is worse.'

One of the guards stepped into my line of sight. 'Want me to get rid of her?'

I stiffened, heart thudding in my chest.

Were they going to kill me?

2

I exhaled slowly, dizzy with relief, when the doctor shook her head.

'Give her a sedative and put her upstairs with the others,' she said. 'I'll do some tests tomorrow, see if she can't be useful somehow.'

'What if she has concussion?' said another voice, a woman. 'Should we be sedating her?'

'Do you think I'm an imbecile? The girl is fine. Now, sedate her and get her out of here. I have real work to do.'

The dark-haired doctor stormed off and another woman came into view, taller and with light blonde hair cut short to frame her face. Her face didn't show any kindness despite her querying my fitness to be sedated.

Without making eye contact, she placed a syringe against my shoulder and depressed the contents. Then she stepped back and I lost sight of her.

I struggled to sit up, to call after her, to find out what was going on, but my head reeled, and I sagged back against the mattress. The bed gave a jolt, wheels squeaking as it started to move. The blonde nurse, or whatever she was, was at the head of the bed, while one of the guards was at the foot as I was wheeled out into a hallway.

Staring up at the ceiling made my dizziness worse. I closed my eyes, not opening them again until I was wheeled into an elevator. It was hard to keep them open. I kept blinking, trying to stay awake, thoughts sluggish.

I had to stay alert, had to get out of there. This wasn't a

hospital. This was something else.

The doctor had mentioned Dr Frankel, the scientist who had kidnapped Angel and the others and planned on turning them into weapons. Father had helped foil his plans, but Dr Frankel vanished, only to reappear to try to kidnap Belinda Gregory a couple of months later. He'd once again escaped, but it looked as if he was still determined to go through with his weapons program.

Somehow, he'd got Anthony to work for him, categorising those the guards brought in according to their ability. If he was here, maybe the other missing men were as well. But it didn't sound as if Dr Frankel was going to be happy with the members of the Order that had been abducted today, me included.

Horror swamped me. He'd be after Angel, Belinda and the others again for sure. I had to warn them, an impossible task when I had no energy to do anything but lie there as the elevator stopped and I was wheeled down a long corridor.

I felt the straps holding me down come free moments before my body was lifted and placed on a soft surface. A blanket was thrown over me, half covering my face. The sound of footsteps and the squeaky wheels of the bed I'd been on faded as I struggled into a sitting position, the blanket falling to my lap. The room I was in was filled with shadows, the only light coming from a small window set high in the top half of the door.

It was hard to stay upright, to keep my eyes open, to think, so I lay back down and let exhaustion carry me away.

Minutes, hours; I had no idea how much time passed before something woke me. The hall lights had been dimmed, only a faint glimmer shining through the window in the door.

I blinked several times, trying to make sense of what I saw.

I was no longer lying down. I was upright, standing beside the bed I'd been sleeping in.

I didn't remember getting out of bed. Was I sleepwalking?

I looked down at myself and held back a gasp. I was glowing, my body shining with an ethereal silver light, as it had back at the compound. I lifted my hand and stared at it, through it. I turned to the bed and saw my body still hidden under the covers, and I leaned down to place an insubstantial hand on my chest to see if I was breathing.

The room swirled, a whirlwind took hold of me and I cried out.

I sat up, back in my body, hands patting my chest to make sure I was breathing and not dead.

I subsided against the pillows, shaking. What had happened to me?

Was it a dream caused by the sedative?

But I no longer felt the drug's effects. The sluggishness gone from my thoughts, I pushed back the covers, slipped out of bed, and padded over to the door. I had to get out of there, find a way to warn Grace and the others that Dr Frankel was once again collecting those with psychic abilities. The hallway beyond was in near darkness, making it hard to see anything clearly. I could make out doors on the other side, all with windows set in the top.

I tried the handle, but it was locked. There was a light switch to the left of the door and I turned it on. The light cast a checked pattern on the floor and I looked up at the ceiling and saw the light fixture was secured behind a wire cage with a padlock attached at one end.

The room had a window, but it was barred, and thick black paint covered the glass. The paint had been applied on the outside, making it impossible for me to scrape any away.

With the window barred, being able to see wouldn't help me to get out of here anyway, so I turned to explore the rest of the room.

Other than the blacked-out windows, everything was white. White walls. White tiles on the floor, stiff white sheets and a scratchy white blanket on the single bed pushed into one corner. A white metal bedside table was beside it, with a drawer on top and a cupboard at the bottom.

When I pulled on the bedside table it didn't move. I crouched and opened the cupboard section, looking in the back to see a number of large bolts. It was attached to the wall.

The cupboard itself was empty, as was the drawer.

I kept looking, peering under the bed and seeing it was also bolted in place. The only things that could be moved were the bedding and pillow. With the bars on the window and the light fixture caged, I didn't think this was a hospital. Not a normal one anyway.

A tiny bathroom was hidden behind a sliding door in the wall opposite the bed. I made use of the facilities and then sat on the bed, legs crossed, and watched the door. Someone had to come and see me sooner or later.

In the old motel Father had bought to house the members of the Order before the compound was built, I'd had plenty of time to practise patience. It had been my job to watch and observe, following Father as he interacted with his followers, all while presenting the image of the perfect daughter.

Silence and obedience. Those were the values Father said I had to embody. Hours had been spent at his side, saying nothing, remaining as still as possible, as he dealt with the myriad of issues that arose when putting together an organisation comprising people with psychic abilities.

It had been my job to take notes during Father's recruiting

sessions, detailing what happened as he carried out tests to determine how strong a new follower was in their abilities. I was deaf, unable to hear mental voices, so I was never asked for my opinion or involved in any of the decision making. But Father had no compunction in using me as his assistant, and to take care of more mundane tasks. He'd said it was the least I could do, to earn my place in the new world order he'd planned to bring about.

I shook my head, pushing thoughts of my old life away, hair falling around my face. I tucked it behind my ears, fingers tangling in the curls. It felt so strange, to have my hair loose. Unconfined. I ran my hands over my scalp, rubbing the sore spots that lingered from the last time I had combed my hair into submission and twisted it into a tight bun.

Father would reprimand me if so much as one wayward curl got out of the bun. But he was gone, his body trampled beneath the rubble of the building he had purpose-built to imprison and convert.

I hoped Grace and Liam were okay. And their friends. They had much stronger abilities than the average member of the Order, and I had to believe they would once again prove to be more than a match for Dr Frankel if he went after them as I feared.

Grace had been visibly upset as she waited for the rescuers to find my unconscious body. Though, I couldn't be sure whether what I'd seen was real or not.

It had to be a dream. How else could I have looked down on myself, watched the paramedics bundle me onto a stretcher and carry me away to the waiting ambulance? It was weird that I'd had a similar dream here. Two in a row, when I had never dreamt anything like it before.

The door to the room opened, pulling me from my thoughts.

128

I jumped off the bed to stand in the middle of the room, eyes downcast, hands behind my back. I could do nothing about my hair. I stilled my breathing, hoping whoever was about to enter would not call me on my state of upheaval. They had to think me innocuous, ordinary, if I was to have a chance of escaping.

'What are you doing out of bed? You shouldn't be awake.'

The blonde nurse from before strode in, a stern expression on her face. She fished in a pocket and pulled out a syringe with a cap on the end. 'I mustn't have given you enough earlier,' she muttered under her breath as she slipped the cap off.

Before I could dodge around her, she grabbed hold of my arm and pressed the syringe into my shoulder, dizziness swamping me as the contents entered my bloodstream. She let go of my arm to replace the cap on the syringe, and then slipped it back into her pocket. Then she pushed me over to the bed and made me lie down.

I didn't resist, body limp, head reeling. She pulled the covers over me as I closed my eyes, listening to her footsteps as she switched off the light and left the room, closing the door behind her.

The sedative surged through my system, pulling me under, but I didn't want to go back to sleep. I needed to escape. I had to get to Grace and Liam.

My body whirled, and I opened my eyes, no longer overcome by dizziness.

I was once again standing beside the bed, my body insubstantial. A ghost. My real body was still on the bed. This time I didn't touch it to see if I was breathing. Instead, I walked to the door and peered through the small window, pressing up to the glass.

My head passed through the door and I shuddered, feeling it ripple through my body as I pushed the rest of the way through. I stood in the hallway, dim lighting overhead showing me a row of doors on either side.

I looked back at the door I had come through. The number 217 was on a sign above the window. No longer sure this was a dream, I set off down the corridor. The next room along was 219. The door was open, the room empty, as was 220 across the hall. I started back the way I had come, and found 218 was empty as well, so I moved to 216. The door was closed, but I slipped through it with ease, the rippling sensation back as the door passed through my ethereal body.

A still figure lay on the bed, a soft snore filling the room. I crept over to the bed and saw short blond hair and the top half of a man's face, but it was too dark to discern any of his features. I reached out to pull the blanket back, to see if that would help, but my hand passed right through it. The man shivered when my ghostly fingers brushed his cheek, eyelids flickering, but did not wake.

I left the room and ventured across the hall to 215.

It was also occupied, but this person had flung the covers back as she slept, lying on her back, and I recognised the thin nose and arched brows of a young woman who had recently joined the Order.

Marie. A little older than me, with the ability to shape water.

Rooms 214 and 213 also contained people I recognised. More members of the Order of the Arcane. People who had been in the church when Father brought the ceiling down. All of them had a minor psychic ability.

When I got to 212, there was no mistaking the man in the bed. He was one of the men Father had ordered to dispose of Grace and the male attendants.

I stepped into the hallway and looked at all the closed doors, sure every one of the rooms contained someone from the Order. None of them had been friends. They had tolerated my presence because I was Father's daughter, but I was not one of them.

I was deaf.

I had no psychic ability.

Didn't I?

Was it possible Father had been wrong about me, and the trauma of almost being flattened by a building had triggered a latent ability?

I looked at my hands, waving them in front of my face. They gave off faint silvery light, as did the rest of my diaphanous body. I twisted to look behind me and noticed the thin rope of silvery light streaming away down the hall.

Following it to the door of my room, I slipped inside. The silver rope arched between me and my physical body. I moved over to the bed and touched my chest, where the rope connected.

The room whirled, and I gave a gasp as I felt myself slide back into my body.

I opened my eyes and lay there in the dark, the effects of the sedative gone from my system once more. But I didn't move in case the nurse saw I was awake and came back to give me more drugs.

How much time had passed while I'd been out of my body? Surely not long enough for the latest dose of the sedative to wear off. The lights were still out, no sound coming from any of the rooms around me, and the thought of lying here for hours made me groan.

Maybe I could explore again?

But I had no idea how I'd got out of my body the first time. Or the second.

No matter what I did, I couldn't repeat whatever it was I'd done to slip out of my body.

I lay there in the dark, getting frustrated, until my eyes grew heavy. I hoped when I woke I would be able to figure out where I was and how to escape.

3

The opening of the door woke me.

I jolted upright, heart pounding as the blonde nurse entered the room and placed a pile of clothes on the end of the bed.

'Get dressed,' she said. 'Breakfast is in ten minutes.'

She exited the room, leaving the door open as I scrambled out of bed and moved to inspect the clothes she had left behind.

I grimaced as I unfolded the bundle and found a pair of white cotton pants and a white T-shirt, along with a pair of white scuffs. It seemed Dr Frankel was no more fashion conscious than Father had been.

I entered the small bathroom, used the facilities and changed into the new clothes. There was no mirror in the bathroom, but I didn't need one to know my hair was all over the place. There were small plastic bottles of shampoo and conditioner in the shower recess, like the kind you would find in a motel.

After wetting my hands, I poured some conditioner into my palms, rubbing them together. Then I finger combed my hair, the makeshift de-tangler making the job a little easier. My scalp was sore by the time I was finished, and I was sure my ten minutes had elapsed. I didn't have a hair tie to put my hair up, so it had to remain down.

My hair felt strange as I hurried to the door of the room and opened it, tickling my face each time I moved my head. Father never let me wear it down in public.

Would I be chastised for it here, when I had no other choice?

I opened the door and stepped into the hall, finding myself amidst a small group of men and women also dressed in white. All of them I recognised as members of the Order, including the four men who had not returned from the aborted attempt to dispose of Grace, Nick and Daniel.

The nurse who had come into my room waited with two other nurses, six of the men in black uniforms at their backs. The guards all carried weapons, and I shuddered as their eyes slid over me. I shuffled along with the others when the blonde nurse ordered us to follow her, our scuffs making swishing sounds as we walked. She led the way to an elevator and organised us into three groups. The first group was ordered into the elevator, watched over by two of the guards and one nurse.

I was in the third group, body tense, one of the guards standing right in front of me. I felt him watching me, waiting for me to do something wrong. It was a relief when the elevator came to a stop and the doors slid open. The nurse led us out and through a large area with tables, chairs and couches. My gaze roamed the room, looking for any avenue for escape, heart plummeting when I saw bars on all the windows.

We passed into another short hall and came to a large dining area. The ones who had come in the first two trips were seated at a long table. The rest of us were led over to them and I quickly took my seat as the man with the bushy beard and glasses entered the room. He strode over to confer with one of the guards, turning around every now and then to scan those of us sitting at the table.

I scrunched down in my seat, not wanting to be noticed.

When he had finished talking he came over and spread his

arms wide.

'My name is Dr Frankel, and I'd like to welcome you to the BioTech Foundation. Your new home. You are now BioTech property and are forbidden from using your ability without express permission from your assigned handler. Any unauthorised use will be severely punished. Do I make myself clear?'

No one moved. No one said anything.

The six guards stepped forward, weapons raised.

'I'll ask again, do I make myself clear?' Dr Frankel's gaze was hard, cold, as he scanned us.

A scurry of nods and quietly spoken yesses sprang up. I nodded, eyes downcast to hide my confusion. Why would the others at the table sit here so meekly? They all had an ability. I knew some of them were telekinetic, like Father, though not as powerful. But together they would be able to wrest the weapons out of the guards' hands with ease, and communicate the plan to each other telepathically. Yet they sat there and did nothing.

Why?

I looked sideways, at the girl sitting next to me, the one who could shape water.

Marie's eyes were dulled, head drooping.

She was drugged.

A quick glance confirmed the others were also affected.

I lowered my eyes, hoping none of the nurses or guards would realise I was wide awake.

After breakfast we were ushered to the large common room and told to take a seat. I headed for a distant corner, avoiding eye contact with the rest of them. The guards placed themselves around the edges of the room, watching us. Four people entered the room, all of them wearing white lab coats, with a guard at each of their backs. The doctors selected a psychic each, though perhaps prisoner was a better term, then they retreated down the hallway and disappeared from view.

The others had chosen chairs arranged in front of the televisions spread throughout the room, but I remained in the corner, feet tucked up beneath me. Head down, I let my curls fall in front of my face, using my hair as a screen to observe everything I could.

If my out of body experience had been a sign of a psychic ability, perhaps I could communicate telepathically with the others and find a way to get all of us out of here.

Conscious of the hard eyes of the guards as they scanned the room, I lifted my head and focused on Marie, trying to send out my thoughts. But no matter what I did, how hard I concentrated, nothing happened. I couldn't be sure if that was because she was drugged or if I was kidding myself about suddenly having an ability. Maybe it had all been a drug-induced dream.

But if that was the case, how could I have known Marie was here before I saw her?

One of the guards near me moved and I flinched, thinking he had noticed what I was trying to do. I hunched in on myself as he spoke into a mic clipped to one shoulder. Two large men in blue hospital scrubs entered the room and rushed over to a group of people gathered in front of the television closest to me. Without hesitation, one of them grabbed the man sitting on the edge of the group and yanked his arm behind him. The man struggled, face going red as he yelled at them to let go, that they couldn't keep him here.

The other orderly surged forward, syringe ready, and stuck it in the man's upper arm.

Moments later he sagged in their arms, face going slack. The two orderlies carried him away, toward the set of elevator doors through which we had earlier emerged.

There was a stillness to the rest of us then, and I could tell the man that had been taken away was not the only one to be shaking off the effects of the drugs we'd been given. But none of them protested as a group of nurses entered the room with bottles of water in one hand and small paper cups in the other, no doubt too scared to do anything when watched over by armed guards.

One of the nurses came over to me.

'Time for your medicine, Rose.' She handed me the paper cup.

Two small pills sat in the bottom.

With the guards watching on, I had no choice but to take the pills, washing them down with the water she handed me next.

'Good girl.'

She bustled away, along with the other nurses, and we went back to waiting.

Shortly afterwards the people in the lab coats returned with their guards. I was one of the next to be selected.

My head was spinning, thoughts sluggish, as I unfolded my legs and got up to follow the woman who had called my name. It was the doctor from the night before, the one who had not been pleased to find out who I was. I wobbled sideways, nearly falling, when I took my first step. Neither the doctor or the guard made any effort to help me. Instead, the doctor pointed down the hall.

'Hurry up. You're wasting time.'

Her voice was cold, brusque. The guard's expression alert but remote. He didn't care if I fell over or not, only that I did what I was told.

I shuffled along the hallway, stopping when ordered to at a door with a sign that read "Dr Joanna Wood".

Fear caused my heartbeat to stutter.

Dr Wood was the woman Father had tricked over twenty years ago, when he'd been approached by the original founders of the Order of the Arcane and convinced to make it look as if his psychic ability was fake. She'd been disgraced, her career ruined, and she'd fled to Easton and set up the Wood Estate, where she had tortured Angel, Andie and Celeste.

No wonder she had not been pleased to see me, the daughter of the man who had ruined everything for her. But she'd been arrested, and locked away in a mental institution, thanks to Father's influence. How could she be here, once again working with Dr Frankel?

The door was open, and Dr Wood brushed past me and took a seat behind a desk. The guard stayed beside the door.

'For goodness sake, girl. Sit down.' Dr Wood's eyes were pinched with irritation.

I hurriedly sat in the uncomfortable plastic seat in front of the desk. I was no longer feeling so unsteady; whatever tablets I'd been given were not as strong as the contents of the syringe used to knock us out. Knowledge of how ruthless this woman was, when it came to those with psychic abilities, had my pulse racing.

'Now then, if you truly are deaf as Anthony said, then this assessment won't take long.' Mouth pursed into a scowl, she picked up a large white card off her desk and held it up.

'What symbol is this?'

I shook my head. 'The card is blank.'

'Don't be stupid, girl. Can you see what symbol is on the other side of this card? The side I can see.'

I shook my head again. 'I'm not psychic.'

I would not say *deaf*. There was nothing wrong with my hearing, just because I couldn't hear the mental voice of those who were psychic. Whatever had happened to me before, slipping out of my body, had to be an aberration, not a new-found ability.

Dr Wood's brows were narrowed as she glared at me. Then she tapped a button on the phone on her desk. 'Anthony, get in here,' she said as she pushed back her chair and stood up.

Ignoring the guard posted near the door, she stalked toward me, slipping a hand into a pocket of her lab coat to pull out a slim black device. The door to the room opened and Anthony walked in.

'Dr Wood?' He looked from her to me and back again, his eyes widening. 'What's going on?'

'I need you to listen, here,' she said, tapping the side of her head.

Before I could make sense of her words, she placed the end of the black device on my leg. Pain ripped through my body as an electric current poured into me.

I tried to scream, to get away, but my muscles had locked up, jaw aching as a strangled groan escaped my lips.

Dr Wood lifted the device and looked at Anthony. 'Anything?'

He shook his head. 'I told you, she's not psychic.'

Her mouth screwed into a bitter smile. 'I thought the same thing about my daughter, only to have her throw lightning bolts at me. This is Mark Davidson's girl. I want to be one hundred percent certain she doesn't have a latent ability.'

She stuck the device against my leg and the volts poured into me again. I slumped sideways, almost tumbling off the chair. There was a brief reprieve as she once again asked Anthony if I had made any sound telepathically, before she hit me again. This time I did fall, slumping to the ground, blinded by tears, hair covering my face as I sucked in air.

My entire body was twitching, shudders rippling through

me. The light dimmed, and I felt someone leaning over me. I tried to tense myself, to prepare to be shocked again, but couldn't move. All I could do was lie there in a quivering heap, waiting for the nightmare to begin again.

'Joanna, is that really necessary?'

Someone grabbed me under the arms and lifted me off the floor. Head drooping, I felt myself being placed back in the chair, a hand on my shoulder to steady me when I began to topple sideways once more.

'Dr Frankel, I need to know if the girl is psychic.'

'I am sure there are ways to determine if she has an ability other than with a Taser.'

'You don't understand, she's Davidson's daughter. She's bound to be as deceitful as he was. This is the only way to be sure she isn't lying.'

My eyes were blurry, making it hard to focus as Dr Frankel moved to stand in front of me. He bent down, grabbing my chin and lifting my head. His eyes bored into mine.

'From the looks of her, if she had any ability you would know about it by now.'

'But—'

'Joanna, enough,' he said, releasing my chin. 'I didn't arrange for your release to have you torturing BioTech property because of a grudge. The girl is clearly incapable of mental communication or anything else. BioTech has no interest in those that do not have an ability.'

Dr Wood glared at me, before turning to Dr Frankel. 'You can't let her go. She'll run straight to the authorities.'

'Not that it would do her any good,' he said with a smirk. 'More troubling would be if she were to join forces with your daughter and her friends. But you're right. We can't release her.'

140

I tensed, the movement sending a fresh wave of agony as I prepared to run. Not that I thought I would get far, not with two doctors, a guard and Anthony in the room.

But I had to try. I would not let them kill me.

4

Dr Frankel tugged his beard. 'Take her to Sub Level 3 and put her in Room 6,' he said, turning to the guard. 'I'll figure out what can be done with her after the others have been assessed. She might not have an ability, but that doesn't mean she won't be able to pass the genetic trait on to any offspring. BioTech needs to ensure a sustainable supply of psychics for the future, after all.'

Still struggling to overcome the effects of being tasered three times, it took a while for the meaning of his words to sink in. Then I fought not to gag. He was as bad as Father, wanting to force breed psychics to further his own goals.

I wanted to shout at him, to tell him I would never be part of something like that, but all that came out was a croak, vocal cords straining with the effort. The guard grabbed hold of my arm and dragged me to my feet. I stumbled along beside him as he pulled me into the hall and led the way to the elevator, determined not to pass out as he inserted a key in a slot below the elevator buttons and selected a level underground. My stomach churned as the elevator dropped, though fortunately it didn't have far to go.

The guard's touch was not gentle as he pulled me down a plain hallway, with three doors on either side. Each door had a window set into the top half, like the ones upstairs, but they also had electronic keypads near the handles.

I was taken to a room with number 6 emblazoned at the top. The door was open, and the guard shoved me toward the bed. Before I could turn around, he had left the room and the door closed behind him. I sagged down on the bed, back against the wall, and for a long moment it was all I could do just to breathe, unable to comprehend what had happened.

Little by little, the quivering in my muscles subsided and I was able to sit up straight. I wasn't ready to trust my legs yet, as I pulled sweat-dampened hair back from my face and looked around the room.

It appeared to be a replica of the room I'd spent the night in, except for a chain hanging from a hook near the foot of the bed. Staring at the manacle on the end of the chain, I shuddered, not sure I wanted to know what it was for. Instead, I forced myself to stand and stumbled over to the tiny bathroom. I splashed water on my face, washing away my tears.

My face was red and blotchy, but it was my eyes that held my attention. Haunted, terrified, I looked exactly like I felt; like someone condemned.

I had to get out of there, and find a way to get to Grace and the others.

Stiffening my spine, I left the bathroom and headed for the door to my room, peering through the window.

The hall was empty. The doors of the rooms I'd passed were all closed.

I couldn't hear anything, and I turned sideways and slumped against the door, cheek pressed against the glass, letting its coolness seep into my body, breath fogging up the window.

Then I caught sight of movement in my peripheral vision.

I turned my head to find the hallway still empty. But I had seen something, I was sure of it.

I looked across the hall, at the room opposite, and gasped.

Someone stared back at me, a man with dark blond hair cut short and stubble coating his chin. He had bright blue eyes in a face that was undeniably handsome, even though his features were drawn, and I guessed he was a couple of years older than me.

He was not from the Order. I had met everyone Father had recruited, and I had never seen him before in my life. I was sure to remember if I had.

Who was he?

He mouthed something, but I couldn't hear anything.

He frowned, pointing to his head.

I shook my head when I realised he wanted to know if I heard him telepathically.

He gave a shrug and disappeared from view.

I waited for him to come back, banging on the window to try to get his attention. He didn't return. Eventually I gave up and returned to the bed. I sat with my back against the wall, knees tucked up to my chest, rocking myself as I contemplated my fate.

A male orderly appeared hours later, with sandwiches in a plastic container and a bottle of water. This time there were no pills. I guess they figured they didn't need to sedate me when I didn't have an ability.

As soon as the orderly left the room I jumped off the bed and bolted to the door in time to see him disappear inside the room opposite, accompanied by two guards. The other prisoner must be considered more of a threat than I was. He appeared in the window again once they had left his room, watching the orderly and guard as they retreated down the hallway, but didn't look my way before moving away from the window.

It was a repeat at dinner time, and as I used the plastic cutlery to cut my meatloaf I wondered who he was and what he had done to cause him to be locked up down here. Was he like me, with no ability but imprisoned because of what he knew? But then, I was sure his pantomime had indicated he'd wanted to talk to me telepathically. Maybe his ability was not one that BioTech could use.

Some of the people Father had recruited had barely been able to lift a piece of paper with their minds or light a match. Others could heal a graze or paper cut. Those as strong as Father had been rare. That was why he'd been so determined to bring Grace's cousin and her friends into the Order.

With only my thoughts to keep me company, and my mind filled with questions it was impossible for me to answer, the passage of time felt endless. When the orderly returned to collect my plastic dinnerware and deliver a set of white pyjamas, I didn't hesitate to shower and then climb into bed. I hoped the next day would provide the answers I sought, or a way to escape.

It almost seemed as if I had just closed my eyes when I was once again pulled out of my body.

This time I was more prepared and didn't bother checking my physical body. It was time to explore. I slipped through the door, stifling a grimace at the weird rippling feeling, sure I would never get used to it.

I didn't head straight across the hall. I already knew Room 5 was occupied. I wanted to check the others.

It didn't take long, as they were all empty, and there was no one on guard near the elevator either. An emergency exit was beside the door, with an electronic keypad the same as the ones securing the doors to the rooms. The BioTech Foundation was serious about keeping me and the other guy locked in.

The hall lighting was dim, but the silvery light coming from my ethereal body was enough to allow me to see where I was going as I headed to Room 5. I peered through the window, careful to make sure I didn't touch it. I didn't want to end up sliding through the door until I knew what I was walking…floating…into.

The guy who had stared at me through the window was lying on his bed, shadows making it hard to see if he was awake or not. From what I saw, his room was identical to mine, though unlike me he wasn't wearing white.

He lay on top of the covers, in dark jeans and T-shirt, feet bare.

With a deep breath, I pushed my way through the door.

There was no response from him, no indication he was aware of my presence. That made sense, seeing as I was not really there and could not communicate telepathically with him. I didn't really understand what was happening, why I was suddenly having out of body experiences, but I would use what I could do to figure out how to escape. With luck, the guy could help me with that, seeing as he must have an ability.

I looked around the room, and discovered his attire was not the only difference between him and me. He had a small desk at the end of the bed, with a plain chair placed in front of it. The desk was covered with books and there was a wooden case about the size of a laptop, with a sketch pad beneath it. That wasn't the only difference. Unlike the bare white walls of my room, his were covered with drawings.

I moved closer, to inspect the drawings, letting out a gasp at what I saw.

Each one, drawn in exquisite details, featured dark and disturbing images of people trapped in nightmarish situations.

'Who's there?'

I spun around at the deep voice, letting out another gasp at finding the guy was no longer lying down, but had sat up, eyes scanning the room.

'I know you're there,' he said. 'I heard you. Who are

you?'

I sucked in a breath.

'Listen, I'm getting real tired of this game,' he said. 'Either tell me who you are or get out of my room.' His brows knotted together, nostrils flaring as he glared at the shadowed corners.

'I'm sorry,' I said. 'I didn't know you would hear me.'

His lips curved into a smirk, dimples appearing in both cheeks. 'So, what, you figured being invisible meant you could just barge into my room and invade my privacy?'

I shook my head. 'I didn't know, wasn't sure any of this was real,' I said. 'I thought I might be dreaming.'

'Yeah, because all the invisible girls dream about sneaking into my room in the middle of the night,' he said as he moved until his back was resting against the wall. 'So, who are you and how is it you can not only be invisible but walk through walls?'

'I'm not sure.' I told him what had happened the night before, when I'd found myself hovering beside my physical body. 'I don't know how it happened, that first time. I just wanted to stay awake.'

'I'm not an expert, but that sounds like astral projection,' he said, leaning forward, eyes gleaming in the dim lighting.

'Astral projection?' I'd heard of it. Father had dozens of books that dealt with paranormal activity, but as far as I knew none of his followers had been able to access the astral plane.

His eyes narrowed. 'You wouldn't happen to have had a near death experience lately? I've heard that can sometimes trigger an out of body experience.'

I nodded, forgetting he couldn't see me.

'Yes,' I said, not wanting to explain the circumstances or dwell on seeing Father's dead body.

'Well then, Invisible Girl, that sounds like an out of body

experience for sure. Now we just have to figure out how to use it to our advantage.' He stood up and moved to the door of his room. 'You need to watch while one of the guards inputs the code into the keypad that unlocks the doors. Then we can get out of here. Do you think you can do that?'

'I'm not sure. I don't know what I can do in this shape.' I looked down at my shimmering, ethereal body. 'I passed through the door to get out of my room.'

He picked up a red ball off his desk. 'See if you can take this from me?'

I reached out to grasp the small red ball, my hand passing through it as well as his palm.

He shivered. 'Did you just touch my hand?'

'Yes. It didn't work.'

'Touch me again.' He put the ball down and held out his hand.

I reached out to take his hand, but this time I stopped short of letting my fingers connect.

His eyes went wide. 'I can feel something,' he said, looking at his hand. He wiggled his fingers, and they passed through my hand, causing him to shiver again.

A shiver swept through my astral body as well. 'How am I going to input a code if I can't touch anything?' I wasn't even touching the ground, my astral body hovering just off the floor.

'Do you have a psychic ability other than astral projection?'

'I'm not psychic. At least, I don't think I am. I can't communicate telepathically.'

He rubbed a hand over his chin. 'Then how are you talking to me now?'

'But I couldn't talk to you, before. Or anyone else.'

He shrugged. 'Maybe it only works when you are in astral

form. Either way, you're talking to me now and you still haven't told me who you are or why you got locked up in the dungeon with me.' He frowned. 'It can't be because they're worried about your ability. Not if all you can do is astral project. This lot are only interested in guinea pigs with useful psychic abilities.' He gave a tight smile. 'So, Invisible Girl, I'm Lachlan Dales. What's your name?'

'Rose Davidson,' I said.

'Nice to meet you, Rose. Welcome to Hell.' He spread his arms wide, voice tinged with darkness. 'Otherwise known as the former Wood Estate, and the new home of the BioTech Foundation.'

'Why are you locked up down here?' I asked. Had he been one of the patients kept here?

'Nah, not me,' he said. 'My previous hellhole was in Sydney.'

I gasped. Lachlan had responded to my thought.

He gave a snort. 'Of course I did. That's Psychic Fun Fact Number One. We can all talk to each other telepathically, once we've made the initial connection. Of course, I didn't find that out until I met Belinda Gregory.'

Belinda. Grace's cousin. The one who had the vision that saw Grace picked to be Liam's mate.

Lachlan screwed up his face. 'Man, I'm getting seriously twisted vibes off whatever it is you're thinking now. Stop it. I've got enough of that already.'

Mind boggling at what he'd said, it took me a moment to realise he hadn't answered my first question. So, I asked again.

'After I helped Belinda, Frankel had me locked up down here. Seems he no longer had a use for me once he discovered I'd burned out and weaned myself off his happy juice.' He tapped the side of his head. 'If I can't see the future for him

149

and his clients, I'm useless to BioTech. Being able to communicate telepathically is the only thing I can do now, and even then, I need to be in proximity or I can't hear a thing.'

His expression lightened. 'Now you're here, I'll finally have the chance to escape. Once we figure out how to get you to interact with physical objects.'

I sucked in a breath, hoping it would be as easy as Lachlan made it sound.

The sooner we got out of here the better.

5

No matter how hard I concentrated, I could not manage to touch anything.

'This is useless,' I said hours later, waving my hands in the air and setting my astral body shaking. 'I can't do it.'

Lachlan's expression darkened, hair mussed from the amount of times he'd gripped it with his hands. 'Don't flake out on me now, Rose. I'm counting on you to get the two of us out of here.' His voice was brisk, matter of fact.

'What about the others imprisoned here?'

'If they're not useful, they'd just be excess baggage. On our own, we have a chance. Trying to rescue the rest would slow us down.'

I frowned. They were Father's followers he was talking about abandoning. I had no friends among them, most of them choosing to follow his lead in ignoring me because I had no ability. But that didn't mean I wanted them hurt.

'If Dr Frankel is planning on turning them into weapons, we have to free them as well. It's not right to leave them here.'

'Look, let's just concentrate on getting you and me out of here for now. Then we can work on freeing the others, okay?'

I was sure he had only said it to mollify me, to manipulate me into doing what he wanted, but he was right about one thing. Until I figured out how to use my ability properly none of us was getting free.

I heaved out a sigh, willing myself to get it together as I eyed the red ball sitting in the palm of Lachlan's hand.

A click sounded behind me, coming from the door.

Lachlan stiffened, fingers wrapping around the ball.

'Get the code,' he said, the intensity of his mental thoughts reverberating in my head. I pushed my astral form through the door, dodging to the left to avoid sliding through the orderly standing on the other side, everything happening too fast for me to see the full code as it was input, the light already changing to green.

Two guards stood just behind the orderly, guns at the ready as he swung the door open.

Lachlan stood in the middle of his room, face deceptively blank. 'Little late for visiting hours, don't you think?'

'Frankel wants to see you.'

Lachlan dipped his chin, a hard smile curving his lips. 'Better not keep the man waiting then.' He stepped over the threshold and strode confidently down the hall, not waiting for the orderly or the guards to catch up.

I moved to follow, curious as to why Dr Frankel would want to see Lachlan in what had to be the middle of the night.

'You don't want to know, Rose. Get some sleep. We'll work on our escape plans tomorrow.'

Lachlan didn't turn around as he made his telepathic suggestion, and I was tempted to ignore him and follow along anyway. But the sense of dread filling his mental voice made me hesitate. Whatever was going on, he didn't want me involved. But whether that was to shield me or him, I couldn't tell.

As he was my only ally, I decided that going against his wishes would not be the best way to go, so I moved to the door to my room. Moments later I was back in my body, weariness swamping me as the lateness of the hour and the mental strain I had been putting myself under hit.

It was a relief to snuggle under the covers and close my

152

eyes.

Tomorrow I would continue to work with Lachlan, to find a way out of here for all of us.

I'd been able to catch the last couple of numbers the orderly had input in the keypad to Lachlan's room. But I'd need to get the ones I'd missed, and figure out how to actually touch the keypad, before I could be of any use to either of us.

Thoughts of what might be happening to Lachlan followed me into sleep, making for a disturbed night. I was bleary eyed, brain sluggish when the door to my room opened and the orderly who had collected Lachlan the night before tossed a fresh set of clothes on the end of my bed.

When I left the tiny bathroom, the door to my room was open, the orderly waiting in the hall. I risked a quick glance toward Lachlan's room when I joined the orderly, but there was no sign of him, the door closed. Either he wasn't back, or he was still sleeping.

There was no time to worry about Lachlan as I was taken to the ground floor and ushered into Dr Wood's office once more. She stood behind her desk, sending baleful looks at Dr Frankel who was sitting in her chair, while Anthony was leaning up against the wall to my left. The orderly directed me to the chair in front of the desk. I sat, casting wary glances at both doctors as the orderly backed out of the room, closing the door behind him.

Dr Wood scowled, like every other time I had seen her.

But it was the smile on Dr Frankel's face that concerned me.

Lips full and fleshy, the beard hiding most of his face, the twinkling eyes behind his glasses seemed out of place in the context of BioTech.

Straightening my shoulders, I stared back at him and his eyebrows rose.

'Well, Rose, how are you settling in to your new home?' he asked, leaning forward and placing his lower arms on the desk.

'This is not my home.'

He pursed his lips. 'I'm afraid we may have got off on the wrong foot. You're not like the others who have become part of the BioTech family. You're special. I should have realised that immediately. I apologise. You should never have been treated so harshly your first day here or thrown in the basement. Dr Wood has been reprimanded and assures me it will not happen again.'

My gaze flicked to Dr Wood when she gave a snort. Her sour expression suggested she didn't believe a word he was saying either. The reason I'd been tasered and then thrown in the basement was because he and Dr Wood believed I was useless.

A chill settled in the pit of my stomach as I figured out what this was about.

They had reason to believe they'd been wrong.

I fought to keep the panic welling inside me off my face. They must know about my new-found ability.

What were they going to do with me?

'Relax, my dear,' said Dr Frankel. 'You are safe here. I just need you to help me with something.'

I shook my head, curls falling forward, and sucked in a deep breath. 'I don't understand?'

'Anthony tells me that you were your father's assistant.'

I looked over to where Anthony leaned against the wall, looking bored with what was happening in the room. His nonchalance did not make me inclined to relax, as I sensed it was as false as Dr Frankel's apology.

'Rose, is that true?'

I pulled my gaze back to Dr Frankel. 'Yes.'

He rubbed his hands together before picking up a thick notebook and a pen. 'That's wonderful.'

He stood and came around the side of the desk, leaning over and handing me the notebook. I took it automatically, scanning his eyes for a sign of what was going on. If this wasn't about my ability, then what did he want? Surely not an assistant?

'I need you to write down all the names of your father's followers and their abilities. Start with the ones who were stronger and work your way down the list.' Dr Frankel gripped my shoulder and gave a squeeze. 'Anthony has given us the names and abilities of those he knows, but you would have more information than him. We will be checking both lists, to make sure there are no inaccuracies in your reporting. Or Anthony's,' he said with a low chuckle as he let go of my shoulder and stepped back.

Notebook clutched in nerveless fingers, I stared up at him as it all sank in.

'No. I won't help you.' Hands shaking, I moved to throw the notebook back on the desk.

He leaned in and gripped my hands before I could do so, squeezing until the pain made me gasp. 'Rose, be sensible now. The world is not a safe place for those with an ability. That is why your father and his mentors built the Order of the Arcane in the first place.'

I shook my head. 'I know who you are. I won't help you turn innocent people into weapons.'

'Innocent?' scoffed Dr Frankel. 'Your father was plotting to overthrow the government, and his followers had agreed to help him do it. How is that innocent?'

I said nothing, aware there was no way to defend what my father was planning to do. And it was true, that many of his followers had been willing to see it through. But that didn't mean I was going to give this man a list of the members his guards hadn't been able to capture. A list of people for him to target. For every person who had believed Father's way was the right way, there were three more who came to the Order because they had nowhere else to go.

Dr Wood shifted, expression souring. 'I told you you'd get nothing from the girl. You might not like my methods, but there is no denying they work.' She reached into her pocket and pulled out the slim black Taser.

I stiffened, eyes widening, looking from her to Dr Frankel. He'd stopped her last time. He wouldn't let her try it again, would he?

His eyes narrowed as he stared at Dr Wood, mouth in a thin line, and tugged on his beard. Then he looked over at me and gave a grim smile.

'I'm sure Rose, now she is aware of the stakes, will be happy to help us without the need to resort to more … extreme methods. Won't you, dear?'

I shook my head, fear of having Dr Wood come near me with the Taser freezing my voice. But if she did, I still wouldn't tell him what he wanted to know. Besides, even if I did give him a list of names, that wouldn't help him. The former members of the Order must have scattered by now.

'Well then, that is a pity,' said Dr Frankel, getting up from his seat. He waved a hand at Dr Wood. 'Let me know what you get out of her.'

A strangled gasp escaped my throat. He was going to let her torture me again.

He made his way around the desk, reaching out to give me a patronising pat on the top of my head. 'This is your last chance, Rose.'

I couldn't answer him, unable to take my eyes off Dr Wood as she drew near, Taser raised up in front of her. I

156

threw myself sideways, off the chair, hearing a shout from Anthony. I felt him lunging for me, but I twisted away, trying to get to the door. Dr Frankel was there, blocking it, and with Dr Wood and Anthony at my back I had nowhere to go.

Something small and hard was rammed into my lower back and a jolt of electricity slammed into me.

With a scream, I felt my legs collapse under me, muscles quivering. My head collided with the corner of the desk on the way down, the thud echoing through my body, but I didn't have breath to cry out, muscles still refusing to cooperate.

Tears filled my eyes as my head hit the ground hard, followed by the rest of my body. I lay there, gasping for breath, pain rendering me immobile. I wasn't sure what hurt most. My muscles and nerve endings from the Taser, the side of my head that had hit the desk, or my back where it had hit the floor.

'Stop.'

The shout from Dr Frankel had me looking up, a fresh scream threatening to erupt at the sight of Dr Wood bending over me with the Taser outstretched.

The Taser inched closer to my chest.

Dr Frankel reached over and ripped it out of Dr Wood's hands.

She spun and glared at him. 'Do you want the information or not?'

'She's bleeding. She took quite a knock and could have concussion. You can't taser her in this condition.'

The look on Dr Wood's face suggested she didn't care what condition I was in, only that she got to hurt me, because of who I was.

'Joanna. No more. Not today.'

I sagged back, eyes stinging. Thanks to my head injury, I got a reprieve. But that was all it was. Dr Frankel's supposed reluctance to hurt me was shown to be false. He didn't really care about me. He was just putting off the moment when Dr Wood could torture me again.

Muscles still twitching, I didn't protest as I was scooped off the floor by Anthony. His touch was surprisingly gentle as he sat me in the seat while the two doctors left the room. He shook his head as he gazed at me, gently lifting my curls from the sticky mess on my temple.

'You need to give them what they want, Rose. It will only make it worse for you if you keep resisting.'

'Is that what you tell yourself, to make you feel better about betraying Father and the other members of the Order?'

He gave a sigh. 'Your father's plan was never going to succeed. He was going to lead the Order to ruin, get every one of us locked up and reviled. At least this way we can be taken care of, treated well if we cooperate.'

'How is being turned into weapons better than what Father planned?'

He gave another sigh but didn't speak as he got up and moved to a box hung on the back wall. A first aid kit.

Taking my cue from him, I remained silent as he tended to the gash on my temple. Once it was bandaged, he escorted me from the room. He took me to the dining room, and I was made to sit at a table in the corner, on the other side of the room from the psychic prisoners.

There were more of them today, five more than the first day I ate breakfast here. They'd been rounded up from wherever it was they had fled to, sold out by Anthony.

All of them wore bemused expressions as they ate their breakfast, drugs rendering them docile as they looked around the room.

No matter what Dr Frankel let Dr Wood do to me, I would not subject anyone else to becoming BioTech property.

I would find a way to free the ones that had already been captured.

As soon as I was taken back to my room I would figure out a way to take astral form and find Lachlan. We had to get out of here. That meant I had to figure out how to use my ability and put it to good use, with luck, before I was tortured again.

6

A number of frustrating hours later, I lay back on the bed, still stuck in my body. Exhaustion set in, my head aching from concentrating so hard as well as the result of the bump I'd received earlier. I closed my eyes, taking slow, deep breaths as I hovered on the edge of sleep.

The whirling followed by a lurch caught me by surprise, my eyes snapping open to find myself hovering beside the bed.

Despite finally having achieved my goal, it was disheartening to know the only time I'd been able to take astral form was when I wasn't trying. That was a problem I would have to work on later. For now, I had to find Lachlan.

When I entered his room I found it empty.

Had he been gone this entire time, or had he been returned to his room and then taken out again while I'd been asleep, or being tortured by Dr Wood?

I floated back into the hall and moved toward the emergency doors, freezing when the elevator gave a ding. The doors slid open and the orderly who had collected me earlier stepped out, a tray containing a packet of sandwiches and a bottle of juice in his hands.

I hurried back to my room, realising it must be my lunch. I'd barely eaten anything at breakfast, still recovering from what had been done to me, so food was welcome. I was about to go through the door when I realised this was the perfect opportunity to find out the code for opening it.

I waited to the side, watching as the orderly transferred

160

the weight of the tray to one hand and punched in the code with the other.

607259.

Excitement fizzed through my astral form. The last three numbers were the same as what I'd seen the guard input into the keypad on Lachlan's door. Could it be that they used the same code for all of the rooms?

I wanted to try it out, to see if my theory was correct, but of course there was nothing I could do in this form. Besides, the orderly had entered the room and was staring at my limp body on the bed.

'Hey,' he said, leaning forward and giving me a hard shove. 'Food's here.'

I slipped past him and entered my body, feigning a yawn when I opened my eyes, so he would think I'd been in a deep sleep.

The yawn became a wince when the pain in my temple returned. I struggled into a seated position as the orderly dumped the tray on the end of the bed and left the room. If he cared that I'd been hurt, was still hurting, and was likely to be hurt even more if I remained here, it didn't show.

Movements stiff, head aching, I got to my feet and scooped up the sandwiches on my way to the door. With the way the walls deadened any sound, the only way to know if Lachlan returned to his room was to keep watch. I ate my sandwich standing up, eyes peeled on the room opposite mine, only taking a quick break to go to the bathroom and then grab the bottle of orange juice.

I had just replaced the cap, when I spied movement down the hall.

Lachlan walked slowly, head down, a guard on either side of him.

He didn't look my way, held back by one guard while the

other one input the code to open his door.

The guard blocked the keypad, so I couldn't see if my theory about them using the same number was correct. But it made sense. How else would the different guards, orderlies and nurses be expected to remember so many codes?

When the guards shoved Lachlan inside his room and locked the door behind him, I tossed the empty bottle of juice on the tray and lay on my bed.

Another frustratingly long time passed before I was on the verge of sleep and managed to slip out of my body. I pushed down irritation with my failure to control my ability as I made my way to Lachlan's room. He was lying on his bed, facing the wall, hunched over.

Was he asleep?

Hurt?

'Now's not a good time, Rose,' he said, voice pitched low.

He didn't roll over; didn't move at all.

'I think I know the code to your door,' I said, hovering in the space beside his desk, hesitating to move closer, yet not wanting to leave.

'Can you touch the keypad?'

'Not yet, but I'm working on it.'

'Then why don't you come back when you can actually make yourself useful.'

His harsh words stung, and I wrapped diaphanous arms around my torso.

'I'm sorry,' I said, voice shaking, his tone bringing back my irritation with myself. I was sure I'd never figure my ability out in time to avoid getting tasered by Dr Wood again.

'What?' Lachlan rolled over and sat up, his blue eyes intense.

I gasped, seeing the dark shadows under his eyes, the

drawn features. He looked terrible.

He grimaced. 'Don't worry about me. I'll be fine. What did that crazy doctor do to you?'

From the looks of it, he'd had much worse done to him. 'It was nothing I can't handle.'

'Rose, don't bother lying. I can feel your pain. What did that bitch do?'

It was my turn to grimace, struggling not to think about how helpless I'd felt when Dr Wood had come at me with the Taser. My earlier bravado about being able to withstand whatever she threw at me rang hollow.

He got off the bed and moved closer to me, eyes narrowed as he scanned the air where I was hovering.

Could he sense me? Tell where I was?

A faint smile curved his lips, only to vanish a second later. 'Tell me.'

'Dr Frankel wants me to give him a list of all the members of the Order, their abilities and how strong they are. I refused, so he let Dr Wood taser me.' I put a hand to my temple, the memory of colliding with the corner of the desk setting my stomach churning, a disturbing sensation in astral form.

Lachlan's expression darkened. 'Give him what he wants. If you don't, he'll let her do it again and again until she breaks you.' His hand crept up to his forehead, and I saw a red mark there. Thin, like a strap. There were more red marks around his wrist. I checked his other hand, finding a matching red band.

He'd been restrained.

Had he been tortured too?

His mouth screwed up in a bitter smile. 'Dr Wood doesn't consider it as torture. She seems to think repeated shock treatment will cancel out whatever I did when I burned out my ability. After all, that's what she and Frankel think triggered her daughter's latent ability.'

'If I give him what he wants, he'll go after the others, imprison them, turn them into weapons.' As firm as my determination was to not give in, I knew Frankel wouldn't give up, not until he'd got what he wanted from me. I was also sure my determination would only carry me so far in the face of repeated torture.

'He'll let her hurt you over and over again. No matter how long you think you can hold out, in the end you'll give him what he wants. You might as well give in now and save yourself pain.'

Trying to not let him sense how my own dark thoughts mirrored his, I said, 'The longer I hold out, the more time I have to figure out how to get us out of here.'

He shook his head. 'You don't understand what it will be like, how far she's willing to go. The next time they take you upstairs, you have to give Frankel the list of names, whatever he wants. It's the only way to keep you safe.'

I dredged up a smile, seeking to lighten the mood. 'Keep me safe? That almost sounds as if you care.'

He moved back, body tensing, expression shutting down. 'I don't care. I just need your mind in one piece, to get me out of here. Once they've lost interest in you, and aren't dragging you upstairs every five minutes, we can focus on getting you to be able to input the code to get me out of here.'

'Really?' My smile became more real.

'You need to get it out of your head that I'm some kind of knight in shining armour, out to save the day. My only interest in you is in what you can do for me. I learned the hard way that getting involved only leads to more trouble for me. I won't make that mistake again.'

Despite his comment, I didn't think he was as bad as he

164

made himself out to be, but I let it slide for now. 'I saw the orderly punch the code in to the keypad on my door. The last three numbers were the same as what the guard used on yours. I think they use the same number. Help me figure out a way to be able to touch the keypad. That's what you want, right? To use me to get yourself out of here? We escape, and Dr Wood can't torture either of us again.'

He huffed out a sigh. 'Fine.'

He pointed at the red ball sitting on his desk once more. 'Fetch.'

Sure he was being rude just to antagonise me, I ignored his attitude and focused on what I needed to do.

I let my sense of him drift away, let everything else go, until only the ball remained in my consciousness. It sat there, unmoving, untouchable. But I would touch it. I would get us out of here. Then Lachlan would see he'd been wrong, that helping someone else was not a bad thing. If it wasn't for him, Belinda Gregory would never have got free of Dr Frankel. He'd done a good thing. Yes, he had paid the price for it, but I was sure once he was free she and her friends would be able to help him to heal.

The guy with green eyes had healed me after I'd been pulled from the ruins of the church.

It might not be a quick fix, and I was sure everything he had suffered at the hands of Dr Frankel and Dr Wood would never be wiped clean, but he would have a chance to make a better life.

If only I could stop letting myself get distracted and stay focused on the task at hand.

I sneaked a quick glance at Lachlan, surprised he hadn't called me on my lack of progress so far, but he was once again lying on the bed. He was on his back this time, eyes closed, but the stillness of his form suggested he was not

165

resting. He, more than anyone, knew what was at stake if I didn't get this right.

I turned back to face the desk, my transparent hand hovering over the ball.

It didn't take me as long this time to get back into my meditative state, firmly squashing all thoughts of the guy behind me.

I could do this.

I would do this.

This time, before I tried to touch the ball I closed my eyes. Concentrating on the way it would feel were I to run my hands over the slick rubber surface, the friction it would cause, I sucked in a breath and made my move.

A slight resistance rippled through my fingers, the shape of the ball so real in my mind I was sure it had worked.

Elation filled me as I opened my eyes.

My hand hovered inside the ball, my elation sapped away at the sight and taking with it the faint feeling of resistance.

'Let me guess, it didn't work,' said Lachlan.

I turned to find him in the same position as before, eyes still closed.

'I almost had it. I'm sure I felt the ball that time, as my fingers passed through it.'

'Near enough won't work. You need to be able to pick the damn thing up.' His tone was harsh, his body still tense as he finally opened his eyes and looked my way.

'I'll try again,' I said, straightening my shoulders. 'I'll keep trying until I get it right.'

'No time. I can sense the orderly out there. You need to get back in your body.'

I spun and moved to peer out the window. He was right, the orderly was at my door, punching in the code. I rushed through Lachlan's closed door and then through mine, getting back to my body and sitting up before the orderly had the door fully open.

His eyes narrowed as he stared at me. 'Let's go,' he said, stepping back and gesturing for me to follow him.

I wiped my hands on my pants legs as I got up and moved to the door, swallowing down dread. Lachlan was at his window, watching as the orderly led me away, the expression in his eyes making a hard knot appear in my stomach. But there was nothing I could do but follow the orderly to the elevator. He was three times my size. I'd never be able to get away from him.

I stood beside him in silence as we travelled up to the ground floor, sure I was going to be taken to Dr Wood's office to be tasered again.

Instead, the orderly led me to a treatment room.

Dr Frankel and the blonde nurse from my first night here waited beside one of the beds.

'Ah, here she is. Come in and take a seat, Rose. Nurse Branigan here is going to check your injury, make sure all is as it should be.'

I sat on the bed, silent as the nurse checked my wound and affixed a fresh bandage. Then she checked my eyes with a slim torch, followed by my blood pressure. After a few more tests she stepped back.

'She's fine,' she said. 'No sign of a concussion.'

'Excellent. Let's get started then.' Dr Frankel moved to a trolley positioned beside the bed and picked up a syringe filled with a clear liquid.

'Seeing as Dr Wood's method has turned out to have disastrous consequences for you, I decided we'll try a different approach,' he said as he turned back to face me, syringe at the ready.

He waved his free hand and the orderly and nurse

instantly moved in to grip my arms, holing me immobile as Dr Frankel moved closer.

'This is going to help you relax, let you see that I'm not the bad guy here,' Dr Frankel said, pressing the end of the needle into my shoulder. 'I just want to help your friends, give them a safe place to live now that your compound has been overrun by the authorities.'

A sharp sting, accompanied by a sensation of a cold liquid flowing into my arm, as he depressed the contents of the syringe into my body did little to distract me from what he meant.

Whatever was in that syringe, he believed it would get me to tell him everything he wanted to know.

I tried to pull away, to slip out of my body to combat whatever the drug was, but dizziness swamped me. The orderly and the nurse laid me down on the bed as Dr Frankel placed the empty syringe back on the trolley. He then picked up a notebook and a pen and leaned over me.

'Now then, let's start with the ones who have the ability to see the future, and then we'll move on to those who are able to manipulate others.'

7

Silent tears leaked from my closed eyes as the orderly scooped me up off the bed. I didn't move, didn't protest as I was carried from the room, too drained to care what happened to me next. In my drugged stupor, nothing mattered anymore. I was done, my brain hollowed out, emotions dampened by exhaustion.

When I was laid down on my bed, I didn't have the energy to move into a more comfortable position let alone attempt to shift to astral form. I let darkness sweep over me, grateful for the reprieve it offered from having to contemplate what I had done.

Hours later, when the orderly returned to dump a tray with a bread roll sitting beside a covered plate on the end of the bed, it took every ounce of willpower I had to force myself upright. If it wasn't for the grumbling of my stomach at the smell of food, I wouldn't have bothered. Lethargy dogging my movements, I pulled the tray close, relieved to see a pasta dish under the cover keeping the meal warm. I didn't think I would have the energy or the coordination to use plastic cutlery on a meal that required cutting up.

As I ate the bland pasta dish, some of the lethargy left my body, though I was still finding it hard to keep my eyes open and my head up. As soon as I finished the pasta, using the bread roll to sop up the remnants of sauce, I leaned back against the headboard to sip the bottle of water.

Once I was done, I placed the empty bottle back on the tray and stumbled to my feet, shuffling into the bathroom.

Then I returned to the bed and curled on my side under the covers, determined to sleep for as long as possible. Maybe then I would be capable of coherent thought and action.

No sooner had I closed my eyes and made myself comfortable than I felt the swirling sensation that indicated I was taking astral form. I wanted to protest, to hunker down in my body and lose myself in sleep, but when I opened my eyes the lethargy had gone, and I was now wide awake, no lingering trace of the drugs that had been pumped into me serving to dull my memory of what had happened.

I looked down at my physical body, contemplating slipping back into it. Not that doing so would help me evade the memories. Still tempted to give it a go, I froze when a pained mental cry echoed in the air around me. I moved to the door and peered out the small window, holding back a cry of my own when I saw Lachlan suspended between two guards.

His head hung down as they dragged him over to the door of his room. One of them released his grip on Lachlan to punch in the code to unlock his door, and then they tossed him inside. I winced as I saw his body hit the ground. He struggled to lift himself, only to fall back to the floor as the guard swung the door shut and cut off my view.

Before I could think about what I was doing, I was through my door and on my way to Lachlan's room. I didn't know what help I could offer, when I couldn't even touch him, but there was no way I could leave him lying there alone.

I hovered on my knees beside him, listening to his ragged breathing as he again attempted to rise. I put out a hand, wishing I could do something, anything, to help as he painfully dragged himself up, muscles in his arms straining, legs shaking.

After a few stumbling steps, he collapsed on his back on the bed, sweat darkening his hair and shirt as he lay there gasping for breath.

'What did they do to you?'

'Nothing I can't handle,' he said, voice raspy.

Tears pricked my eyes at his use of the same phrase I'd said to him, after I'd been tasered by Dr Wood. No matter what he said, he couldn't take much more of this.

He grimaced. 'Seems Frankel didn't like the answers you gave him. He wants a working seer as soon as possible and doesn't care how many times Dr Wood zaps me if it will bring my ability back.'

Shame fizzed through me to know he was aware I'd given Dr Frankel the names he'd wanted, and what I knew of the strengths of each member of the Order while under the influence of the drug he'd injected me with. Like Father, he had appeared unimpressed to learn they had limited success with seeing the future or in getting others to see or do what he wanted. That was why Father had been insistent on adding Liam Devine and Belinda Gregory to the Order.

Lachlan rolled onto his side, though it was evident the movement cost him in energy and pain. 'Look, it wasn't your fault. Frankel's patience was running out before you got here. From what I figure, he's planning something big and wanted surety it would work, or at least that he would have the means to make sure it did.'

'What do you think he's planning?' I asked, not convinced I should be let off the hook that easily.

'I don't know, but we need to find out. I want you to head upstairs and scope the place out, see if you can get an idea of what it is he's planning. We're flying blind here.'

'Okay,' I said, not at all sure if I should leave him. But the best way to help him would be to find a way to get him out of here. He couldn't take much more of this kind of torture before it broke him completely.

171

I stamped down on my fear for Lachlan and slipped through the door, floating down the hall as I tried to figure out how to get my astral body to go up.

So far, I had only floated along just above the floor. I eyed the elevator doors for a moment, not sure what would happen if I slipped through them and then tried to float through the roof and up the elevator shaft. A shiver swept through me at the thought of getting trapped in the dark shaft, cut off from my body forever.

Then I looked to the left and spotted the emergency exit.

With a sigh of relief, I made my way through the locked door and started up the stairs. It felt strange, not really walking but still managing to climb as I reached each step. I continued up to the ground floor and left the stairwell. The door on this end did not have a keypad on the inside, but I checked to see there was one on the outside.

The guard had used a key to get the elevator to go to the sub level. To escape we would either need the key or hope the code to my room worked here too, and for any other doors between the sub level and the exit.

First though, I had to find out more about what was going on in this place.

The ground floor offered no clues. The common room was empty, as were the treatment rooms, offices and storerooms behind it.

The dining and kitchen area were still and quiet; no sign that any of us had ever been here with the tables wiped clean and the benches spotless.

I headed down the hallway and came to another door locked with a keypad.

This door led to a large reception area with big glass windows. As with the rest of the space, only dim lights were on, but the windows allowed moonlight to stream it as I went to the reception desk to see what I could find.

The desk was as clean as everything else; the drawers and cupboards behind it closed. With my astral body unable to move anything other than myself, it was impossible to check their contents. Annoyed with the lack of information, I turned to go back to the stairwell, to go up to the next level to see what I could find.

A movement in my peripheral vision brought me to a halt.

Slowly, I turned my head and spotted two guards roaming outside the building, weapons in their arms as they patrolled. As I watched, one of them came to the glass front doors and shone a torch inside.

Panic swamped me, making my ethereal body shake, until I remembered that no one could see me. After panning his torch light over the room, the guard moved on with his partner and I headed back to my searching, frustrated by my inability to find anything to say why Dr Frankel was so insistent on having a strong seer and someone capable of mental manipulation of others.

When I ventured up to the floor where I had stayed on my first night here, I had to stop my search a number of times as nurses and orderlies checked on their prisoners, some of them with guards in tow. More guards patrolled the corridors on this level as well and I froze, not daring to make a sound when I passed any of them in case they might hear me.

I also tried to keep my mind blank as I checked on the other prisoners. Lachlan had been able to hear my thoughts, so they might too. But I soon found that none of them was capable of doing much. All of them were asleep, and from the vigilance of the nurse who had drugged me, I didn't think their slumber was entirely natural.

There was no sign of the doctors, so they must stay somewhere else, but there were plenty of night staff left behind to make it hard for any of us to escape.

I headed to the ground floor, and down the hall toward the back door I had spotted earlier. If I did find a way to input the code and it worked on all doors, I needed to know what else we would have to deal with to enable us to escape.

What I found outside had my spirit wilting.

Armed guards patrolled the premises, roaming in sets of two. I saw four sets at least as I followed a dirt road to a gate in the back fence. Two more guards waited in a guard post that looked to be fairly new. Dr Frankel was taking no chances on any of us escaping.

Or were the guards there to keep others out?

Either way, it was going to make it almost impossible to get one person out of here let alone all of us.

I was going to explore more but a flurry of activity outside made me rethink my plan. The gate opened, and a van was driven through, coming down the dirt road to the back entrance at a fast pace. It skidded to a halt and a guard jumped out of the passenger seat and raced to open the back door of the van.

Anthony, dressed in black like the guards, leaped out and then turned to face into the van, arms up as he assisted a pale-faced Marie to clamber out. Her body was shaking and I heard her teeth chattering as she struggled to remain upright.

'He's dead,' she said, her voice a wail. 'Why did you make me do that?'

A nurse rushed past me, syringe ready, and within moments Marie was unconscious, slung up in Anthony's arms as he and the nurse hurried inside.

The guard at the back door watched them disappear down the hall before turning to the one who had jumped out of the van.

'I take it the mission was a success?'

The guard grinned, teeth gleaming in the headlights. 'Sure was. The target didn't know what hit him, when the water in his bath went crazy. With no witnesses, and no marks on the body, no one will ever know his drowning wasn't an accident.'

I gasped, suddenly understanding Marie's words.

They'd made her kill someone using her ability.

The first guard's grin was as wide as the others. 'Frankel will be pleased. With the target out of the way, that's one less obstacle we'll have to deal with. Which is good news for us.'

'Yeah, but I hope he doesn't let the psychics have all the fun,' said the second guard, caressing the butt of the pistol in a holster at his waist. 'Being a babysitter is boring. I want some action.'

'There'll be plenty of action to go around if what Frankel said about that taskforce was true. They'll continue to make trouble, for sure, if they find out what's really going on here.'

'They give us any trouble, we'll just have one of the psychics take them out,' said the guard with a shrug. 'No big deal.'

Horrified by their callous disregard for the lives of others, I retreated down the hallway. I had to go back and tell Lachlan what I had heard. It was vital we escaped, so we could find the taskforce and warn them, and find a way to stop Dr Frankel using Marie and the others to kill people.

I couldn't begin to imagine how she must feel, the guilt that would be eating away at her for what she had been forced to do. How had they controlled her, when she could have easily turned the water against them?

When I returned to the room, Lachlan still looked weak and exhausted but was sitting up at least. His brow creased as he listened to what I had discovered.

'It's not the first time Frankel has used a psychic to do his dirty work,' he said. 'This taskforce must be causing huge problems for BioTech for him to resort to murder though. Maybe that's why he wants a seer, to keep one step ahead of them.'

I remembered what the guard had said, about there being no witnesses and no marks to show the drowning had not been accidental. Then I thought of the people from the Order who had been kidnapped.

'He's going to turn them all into killers.'

'Maybe, maybe not. Not all the jobs he gets us to do involve death.'

I floated closer. He'd said "us".

'Has he made you kill people too?'

His expression darkened, and he lowered his head.

I didn't think he was going to answer me and was sure I wouldn't like the answer if he did.

Finally, he lifted his head and said, 'No. I haven't had to kill anyone, but I've done a lot of other stuff.'

'I don't understand how it happened,' I said. 'I mean, Marie could have turned the water against the guards and got away. She wasn't drugged, or she couldn't have been able to do what she did. So she could have fought.'

'You'd think so,' he said, voice bitter. 'But sometimes making the right choice is hard, especially when Frankel's happy juice is involved.'

He'd mentioned happy juice before. I thought he'd been referring to the sedatives the others had been given to block their abilities. But from the bleak expression in his eyes I guessed I was wrong.

'What does it do to you?'

He ran a hand over his face. 'Nothing good. It's addictive, and it causes intense headaches when you don't get the next dose in time.'

176

'That's horrible.'

'Tell me about it. He started me on the stuff six years ago. Told me it was to stop the pain I got when I had visions. Didn't tell me it would make the pain worse.'

'Six years. But you would have been just a child.'

'I was fourteen and thought I was bullet proof. Until I had my first vision, and saw my parents die in a car accident. Thought it was some kind of nightmare, until it came true.' The bleakness in his eyes deepened.

'I'm so sorry.' I floated closer, lifting a hand, wishing I could offer more than words as comfort.

'You've got no reason to be sorry. You weren't the ones who ditched me when I told them what I'd seen. You're not the one who stuck me in a group home while they tried to figure out who should have custody of me.'

He gave a harsh laugh. 'Of course, when I told them the place was going to go up in flames they didn't believe me. When it happened, just the way I'd said it would, I got the blame and they threatened me with juvenile detention. That's when I split, took to the streets. Frankel found me not long after, gave me my first dose of his happy juice after telling me it would help make the visions go away. I was so desperate to believe him, I swallowed it down without a protest.'

He shook his head. 'Six years later I find out the bastard tricked me, turning me into a junkie to get me to do his dirty work for him. But no more. I'm no one's puppet. Soon as I get out of here, no one will ever trick me again.' His voice was harsh, face twisted into a grimace, and for the first time I got a sense of the pain behind his anger.

Not physical pain. Emotional. Everything he'd been through since the death of his parents had left its mark.

Knowing that made it easier to understand why he wasn't concerned about the fate of the others. He just wanted to be

177

free.

I wanted the same but couldn't forget the horrified look on Marie's face as she contemplated what they'd made her do.

The others would also be made to do horrible things to satisfy the needs of Frankel's clients. I couldn't just walk away from them.

Not that I had a means of escape yet anyway.

Perhaps disturbed by what he had shared, Lachlan closed himself off from me, and I lost the sense of his feelings.

'You'd better head back to your body and get some rest. Tomorrow we'll work more on getting you to control your astral form. You should be safe from being tasered, at least, seeing as Frankel got what he wanted from you.'

I might be safe, but what about Lachlan? If Dr Frankel was still determined to revive his ability, he could be subjected to more torture. But from the closed off expression on his face, and the dark thoughts rolling off him, he was well aware of that and didn't want to talk about it. I didn't protest when he again urged me to get some rest, everything I had discovered weighing me down as I left his room and returned to my own.

I had a feeling when morning came it would present a new host of problems to solve, not least of which would be convincing Lachlan we needed to take the others with us.

No matter that it would make escaping much harder, I would not stand by while innocent people were used to do the dirty work for BioTech.

8

Morning came before I was ready for it. A nurse bustled into the room, with a guard at her back.

'Hurry up and get dressed,' she said as she dumped a fresh pile of clothes on the end of the bed, along with a pair of slip on shoes. 'Your exercise session is in ten minutes.'

She left the room, closing the door behind her as I jumped out of bed. I scooped up the clothes, wiping sleep from my eyes with my free hand as I hurried into the bathroom. I changed, washed my face and ran my hands through my hair before the door to the room opened.

'Rose, hurry up.' The nurse's voice was brusque.

'Coming,' I said as I hurried out of the bathroom and slipped the shoes on.

In the hall, I came to a halt when I spotted Lachlan with a guard on either side of him. He was still wearing the jeans and shirt from the night before, teamed with a pair of sneakers. Exhaustion wreathed his features, shoulders slumped, but he straightened up when he saw me.

'So, you're the new girl,' he said, his voice a weary growl. 'Welcome to Hell.'

Horrified by how bad he looked and sounded, it took me a moment to understand why he was acting as if he didn't know me, but then it clicked. The guards, and the nurse, would not expect us to have met each other before. Locked in separate rooms, with me supposedly unable to communicate mentally with anyone else, we should be strangers. I wasn't supposed to know the reason he looked as if he'd been hit by a truck.

I gave him a nod in greeting but didn't want to say anything with the others watching on.

'Get moving,' said one of the guards.

Lachlan gave him a black look but said nothing as he started walking down the hall at a slow pace, movements stiff. From the way my muscles and nerve endings had protested long after being tasered, I knew it had to be ten times worse for Lachlan. Yet despite the pain he must be feeling, he appeared relaxed, unconcerned with having an armed guard at his back.

They were there to watch him, not me.

Even the nurse seemed to be wary of him. She kept a hand in her pocket during the ride to the ground level, and I was sure she had hold of a syringe, ready to pump a sedative into him if he made a wrong move.

But Lachlan did nothing unexpected as we were led through the empty common room, to the back entrance I had explored the night before.

No one was around; the hallways and rooms we passed were all empty, pale light streaming through the windows. It was early morning, just after dawn, so I guessed everyone else was still asleep. Everyone except for the guards on duty that was.

Two were by the back door when we exited, and more patrolled the grounds. The two guards with us led us along the dirt road for a time and then verged left instead of heading to the gate. Here there was an empty patch of grass bordered by trees. I saw the remains of what looked like a garden, with concrete slabs indicating some kind of structures had once sat there.

The guards took up position at the tree line, the nurse at their side. She pointed to the grassed area. 'You have thirty minutes. Don't waste it.'

Movements smoother now, Lachlan immediately set off, taking a circular path around the edge of the clearing. I hurried to catch up with him, scanning the guards who had stopped whatever it was they had been doing to watch us.

With so many eyes looking on, I was hesitant to say anything about what had happened the night before.

'They treat me like an animal,' said Lachlan, after we had completed two laps, anger ringing in his low voice. 'Take me out for a daily walk and then lock me up again. But never when any of the others are out in case they start to get ideas about disobeying their master. We need to get out of here. I can't take much more of this.'

'How are we supposed to escape?' I said, voice pitched low. 'You've seen how many guards there are. It was the same last night. Even if we could get out of our rooms and figure out a way to get upstairs and outside, we'd never make it far before we were spotted. Not without help.'

He cast a quick glance my way, eyes hooded. 'What are you thinking?'

'I know you don't want to involve the others, but we could use their abilities to aid in our escape.'

He shook his head. 'They're drugged each night, and how would we get them to agree to even plan an escape?'

'I could talk to them, as I did you, when in astral form. I could do it later today, before they're given their night dose.'

'There are over a dozen of them. And what if one of them ratted you out? They'd start you on the drugs too.'

The thought of being drugged and turned into a weapon like Marie was terrifying, but then I didn't think astral projection was the kind of thing that could be weaponised. 'I need to try,' I said.

Before I could say anything more, the nurse called out that exercise time was over. She and the guards returned us to our rooms. Before the door was locked behind me, an orderly delivered a breakfast tray. I ate quickly, not wanting to waste time. Yesterday they hadn't taken away the dirty dishes until the next meal was delivered so I figured I was fine to work on controlling my astral projection.

I needed to be able to do it at will, not wait until I was almost asleep.

I had just made myself comfortable when the door to my room opened, setting off a rising tide of panic. What if Lachlan had been wrong, and I was going to be taken upstairs and drugged or tasered again?

I jerked upright and watched as the orderly tossed a pile of books onto the end of my bed before scooping up the breakfast tray.

Heart still thudding, I lay back down. I had to figure out how to use my ability properly. I couldn't wait until night, when I was on the verge of sleep, to talk to Lachlan and the others. We had to make plans, to figure out how to get out of here before Marie was forced to kill again, or any of the others were made to do the same.

I took a deep breath, closed my eyes and exhaled slowly, focusing on my breathing while thinking about what it was I wanted to achieve.

I pictured my ethereal body, silver and shimmering.

Gradually I felt my body grow heavy, entering almost a meditative state as I breathed in and out slowly, my body relaxed, mind disconnected.

Then the heaviness was replaced by weightlessness.

I opened my eyes and smiled.

I'd finally done it. I'd taken astral form on my own terms.

Without delay, I slipped through the door, the rippling sensation barely bothering me this time. Then I rushed to Lachlan's room, eager to tell him what I had done.

I passed through his door and froze, open-mouthed, eyes wide.

Lachlan was half-naked, on the floor, doing push-ups, jeans riding low on his hips. The muscles in his toned back flexed as he dipped down and then pushed himself back up. He held the position for a moment, the gleam of sweat glistening on his upper body. Then he repeated the movement.

A quiver swept through me at the sight, and I was thankful I was in astral form as I was sure I'd be blushing. Not that he would see me anyway, with his body facing away from me.

He did three more push-ups and then stood, reaching to a towel placed on his bed to wipe the sweat from his body as he turned around and scanned the air in front of him.

'Enjoy the show?' A faint smirk curved his lips.

Oh God, he knew I was there.

I wanted to flee, to pretend I hadn't been watching him, practically drooling, but that would surely make the situation even more embarrassing.

Instead, I lifted my chin and said, 'I'm just surprised you wanted more exercise. You didn't seem impressed with our walk.'

'I may object to being treated like a dog, but I do want to remain fit,' he said, throwing the towel on his bed. He picked up his discarded shirt and slipped it back on, covering a torso that was just as toned and impressive as his back.

'Anyway, I just came to tell you I was able to slip into the astral plane without falling asleep this time. It's the first time I've been able to consciously do it.' Pride at what I had accomplished flushed away the last of my embarrassment.

'That's great. Now you just have to figure out how to touch me,' he said holding out his hand.

A quiver worked its way through my body at his words. I

stared at his offered hand, but that wasn't what I was imagining myself touching as an image of his toned torso entering my mind. I pulled my gaze away, when he began to smirk again, and looked over at his desk.

'I think I should stick with inanimate objects for now,' I blurted out when the silence had gone on for too long. I would also have to practise keeping my thoughts to myself when I was around him.

For now, I floated over to the desk and focused on the red ball I'd tried to touch the day before. Just as I had controlled my breathing before slipping out of my body, I inhaled and exhaled slowly. Even though I wasn't really breathing, not in this form, the action helped to ground me as my gaze centred on the ball. At first all I felt was a shimmer, more of a sensation of drifting in the astral plane, as I prepared myself. Then, slowly, the sensation of movement in my diaphanous form settled until I had achieved almost complete stillness.

I reached out a hand, not daring to even fake breathe as I touched the ball.

'Hey, Invisible Girl, are you still here?'

My fingers slipped through the ball and into the desk at Lachlan's voice.

I spun around and glared at him, annoyed that he couldn't see it. 'Do you mind? I'm trying to concentrate here. And my name is Rose, not Invisible Girl.'

'You work out how to manipulate a solid object while in the astral plane and I'll call you whatever you want,' he said, voice pitched low and husky.

A shiver swept through me that had nothing to do with what he'd said, but the way he said it, his deep voice resonating inside my spirit.

I cleared my throat. 'I'd appreciate it if you remained quiet. It takes a while for me to get in the right frame of mind to attempt this.'

'Sure thing ... Rose. I'm shutting up now.'

Humour simmered in his voice, but I turned away from the smile in his eyes and focused on the ball once more.

This time it did not take me as long to get into the meditative state I had achieved before. My fingers swept across the ball and I was sure I felt the edge of it. It felt real, solid, as though I could just pick it up and bounce it.

But when I tried to do just that my fingers passed through it again.

I gave a low growl, swiping my hand at the ball over and over again, frustration swirling as I failed to connect with it.

'Didn't go so good, huh?'

'I felt it. I'm sure of it. But when I tried to pick it up nothing happened.' At least, I thought I'd felt it. Maybe it had all been my imagination, conjured up by the strength of my visualisation.

'If at first you don't succeed, well, I'm sure you know the rest.'

I heaved a sigh. 'Not as though I have anything else to do other than stare at bare walls.' The orderly had brought me books, but I doubted he'd chosen anything I would want to read or that I would be inclined to immerse myself in a story when so much was riding on me learning to manipulate solid objects while in astral form.

I couldn't understand how Lachlan could be so laidback today, after having been practically electrocuted by Dr Wood the day before. It was as if he'd put it out of his mind. Though, with the way my muscles twitched every time I remembered being tasered, I did wonder if his behaviour was an act, a way to lessen the pressure I felt to get this ability of mine under control.

Of course, I was feeling more than enough pressure for

the both of us. No matter how much I practised I couldn't get back to the same state of mind where I felt the ball.

'It's no use. I must have got it wrong, before.' It had to have been my imagination that had made me think I'd succeeded in touching it the first time.

'Why don't you take a break? The orderly will be returning with our lunch soon, so you need to be back in your body before then. After that you can go exploring again, see what's been happening upstairs.'

Lunchtime already?

It didn't seem right, that so much time had passed. I didn't feel hungry or thirsty in this state, but Lachlan was correct about me needing to be back in my body before the orderly came. I did not want anyone entering my room when my body was in such a defenceless state. I had no way of knowing if anyone had been there while I'd been focused on trying to touch the ball.

A fresh surge of panic sent me through the door and back to my room, calling out a hasty goodbye to Lachlan.

'Relax, Rose. No one's been down here. I've been keeping a mental eye on things while you were occupied with trying to touch my ball.'

Warmth flooded me as I slipped into my body, not missing the double entendre of his words.

His husky laugh followed me into my body, ringing in my ears as I blinked and sat up.

Oh God, facing him for real next time was going to be so embarrassing.

9

I was pretending to read one of the books when the orderly arrived with lunch. Back in my body, hunger pangs had started almost immediately so I soon demolished everything on my plate. Once I was done I lay back down, with the book propped open on my stomach to make it appear as if I had fallen asleep reading it. Then I slipped free from my body, amazed at how much easier it was to take astral form this time around. My practice with the ball may not have worked, but at least I now knew how to do one thing right.

I floated into the hall and over to Lachlan's door. I didn't go in. He was standing on the other side, looking through the window, eyes scanning the air where I hovered. He wouldn't be able to see me, but it appeared he sensed where I was because he telepathically wished me good luck before disappearing from sight.

I moved down the hall and to the stairwell, this time stopping at the floor directly above to see if anything was happening there. Shakes flooded through my astral form when I discovered Marie strapped to a bed in the first room I came to. Electrodes were attached to her head with sticky pads, and Dr Wood stood beside her fiddling with a dial on the machine Marie was hooked up to.

A guard stood beside the closed door, eyes narrowed, stance vigilant.

Giving the guard a wide berth, I moved farther into the room, slowly approaching the bed, dread swirling within my translucent form. Marie's eyes were closed, tears leaking from the corners to soak the white sheet beneath her and a thin strap of leather in her mouth.

'Please, I can't take it anymore,' she said, her mental voice throbbing with pain and sorrow as she gazed up at Dr Wood.

With no psychic ability, Dr Wood couldn't hear Marie's impassioned plea, not that I thought she would have cared either way. She flicked a switch and I held back a scream when Marie's body arched upon the bed, eyes rolling back in her head as every part of her twitched and shook. Waves of agony rolled off Marie as the electrical current surged through her again and again.

'Stop it! You're killing her.' I lunged at Dr Wood, desperate to make her stop, but my astral form slid into hers. Dr Wood gasped, and I felt her body stiffening around me, the sensation ten times worse than when I slipped through doors.

I pushed through, shuddering as I came out the other side. I never ever wanted to do that again. Spinning around, I watched as Dr Wood leaned over and turned off the machine she was using to torture Marie. It was the same machine she must have used to torture Lachlan under the guise of trying to revive his ability.

Dr Wood backed away from the bed, scanning the room with narrowed eyes.

I sucked in a breath. Had she heard me call out?

With only my experience with Lachlan to go on, I wasn't sure if it was only those with a psychic ability who heard me when I was in astral form.

I checked on the guard, but he hadn't moved from his post near the door.

Dr Wood gave a shake and then rubbed her bare arms as she moved to the empty bed beside Marie's. She scooped up a lab coat draped across the side rail and put it on. On the other bed, Marie lay still and silent, and I feared it was too late for her, that Dr Wood had killed her.

But as the doctor removed the gag and began pulling off the sticky pads keeping the electrodes in place, Marie gave a soft groan. Her eyelids fluttered, fresh tears spilling from her eyes as she stared up at Dr Wood.

I moved closer, wanting to comfort her. Could I risk it, with Dr Wood and the guard nearby?

As much as I wanted to help Marie, fear of what would happen if she inadvertently let them know someone else was in the room kept me silent. Being tortured with the Taser had been bad enough. I did not want to end up strapped to the bed while Dr Wood electrocuted me. The knowledge that Lachlan had been subjected to the same thing numerous times had my ethereal stomach churning.

Guilt swamped me as I watched Dr Wood undo the straps holding Marie down and ordered the guard to take her back to her room. Later, when Marie was alone and had recovered from her ordeal, then I would go to her and see if I could comfort her. Though I couldn't imagine what help I could give to someone who had just been tortured. Nothing had seemed to work for Lachlan, other than denial.

I needed to find a way out of here, for all of us, so this never happened again.

Conscious of a feeling that time was running out, I headed to the next level. This one was empty, so I continued up to the ground floor. Many of the former members of the Order were clustered around the televisions in the common room, their eyes dull. The same movie was showing on all the screens, with no ads. BioTech wouldn't want its prisoners to know what was happening in the world beyond the estate, the deprivation of current news and affairs surely deliberate. My father had employed a similar technique, keeping newly recruited members isolated until he was sure of their loyalty.

Nothing else was happening on the ground floor, other than guards watching over the prisoners, and nurses and orderlies bustling about as they carried out their duties. It was the same in the upper floors, a few prisoners lying in their beds, either drugged or asleep. I hated to think they may have also been subjected to the same torture as Marie or were recovering from being sent on a mission.

There was no sign of Dr Frankel, though a number of people in white coats or business attire roamed the facility.

With nothing to show for my exploration, I decided to once more venture outside to see if I could work out a pattern to the guards' patrols, for when we were ready to escape. Before I got far a jolt shook me in mid-air. The jolt came again, and I felt my astral form being pulled back the way I had come, streaking through the air. I cried out, twisting to free myself from whatever had hold of me, but nothing worked.

I heard a mental shout from Lachlan, fear surging along with it, but couldn't focus on what he was saying as I was pulled through walls and floors and back to my room. I dimly registered that someone leaned over the bed I was on before I slammed down into my physical body.

A scream ripped out of my throat as the remnants of an electric current surged through my body. I tried to sit up, but hands pushed me back down. Nerve endings quivering, I opened my eyes, raising my arms to strike out at the person restraining me.

It was Dr Wood, an orderly at her back while a guard was watching on from the doorway.

'I thought she wasn't being sedated,' she said, frowning over at the orderly as she pocketed her Taser.

Horror swamped me as I realised she must have used the

Taser on me when they couldn't wake me up. That was the jolt I'd felt before being drawn back to my body. I eyed her warily as she moved back from the bed, arms crossed in front of her chest.

'She's no good to me if she's half-unconscious,' she said. 'I need her alert and receptive for testing to be able to get any useful data from her.'

'She's not sedated. I don't know what was wrong with her. Maybe she was just in a deep sleep when we came in,' said the orderly.

'Perhaps,' said Dr Wood, turning to stare down at me, a speculative expression in her cold gaze. 'But it appears she is wide awake now. Take her to the treatment room and get her plugged in while I check on Lachlan.'

Fear robbed me of a voice when the meaning of her words sank in. She was going to electrocute me, the same as she had done to Marie. I didn't know what data she hoped to get from it, and I really didn't care. I would not let her torture me.

When the orderly moved to the side of the bed I kicked out at him, desperate to keep him away. He blocked my kicks, grunting when I resorted to my hands and tried to punch him.

'Stop that,' he said. 'Before I make you stop.'

I ignored the threat, yanking free and bolting for the bed, searching the room for anything I could use as a weapon. But all I had were books, which he knocked aside easily when I pelted them at him.

He backed me in a corner, using his heavier bulk to subdue me, twisting my arms behind my back as he forced me to walk out of the room.

Tears sprang to my eyes at the pain in my shoulders and I cried out, but he didn't stop, didn't relent. I was shoved into the elevator, made to face the wall. But when he let go with one hand to push the button for the next floor up I used his distraction to wrench free from his grasp and bolted out of the elevator just as the doors began to close.

Hair covering my face, sweat and tears making it stick to my skin, I didn't see the guard until I barrelled right into him.

He forced me back to the elevator to where the orderly waited. Shoved into the corner, gasping for breath, a soft keening noise coming from deep within, I could do nothing as the elevator took me to the next level.

Minutes later I was strapped to the same bed Marie had been on a short time ago.

Something hard was placed over my forehead. No matter how much I moved my head I couldn't dislodge it. I was yelling, telling them to let me go, but no one listened as Dr Wood entered the room and started attaching electrodes to my head.

I pleaded with her, almost desperate enough to tell her what I could do just so she would stop. But I managed to stop myself from blurting out that I had an ability.

She stepped back, and I thought she'd listened, that she was going to stop.

Then the orderly gripped my chin in one hand and forced my mouth open. He inserted the gag with such force I was sure my lips would be bruised. Saliva filled my mouth and I was sure I was going to be sick as I tried to communicate my increasing discomfort to Dr Wood.

The jolt caught me by surprise, scouring away my hope as the electric current burned through my body. The pain was like nothing I had ever experienced before, making the Taser incidents pale in comparison.

Then it was over. I sagged back on the bed, eyes closed.

Dr Wood leaned over me, peering into my eyes with a small torch.

I flinched, trying to pull away from her, the straps holding me immobile.

She moved back and the current surged through me again, even stronger this time. My body twitched, eyes rolling back, heels drumming off the bed, screams strangled by the gag.

I felt a snap, like the one when I had been trapped in the rubble under the church with Father's dead body, and the scream I had been unable to utter vocally filled the air around me as the pain forced me into the astral plane.

Dr Wood crouched beside the bed, hands over her ears, the orderly doing the same at her side as the sound of my scream echoed around us.

The scream faded away, and Dr Wood cautiously lowered her hands as she straightened up, glaring at my physical body.

'I knew she was lying about not having an ability,' she said to the orderly, pointing to the machine set up near the head of the bed.

It had a wide ream of paper coming out of it, with a series of lines in an up and down pattern all over it. Most of the peaks were small, but the ones near where the needle sat were high, almost to the top of the page.

Dr Wood gave my body a shake, and then gripped her fingers into my shoulder so hard I saw the skin whitening under her touch. It would bruise, I was sure of it.

I felt none of it, safe in the astral plane. But I couldn't stay here forever. She knew I had an ability. I had to get out of there, but my body was still strapped to the bed.

'Wake her up.' Dr Wood pointed at the orderly. 'Give her a shot of adrenalin if you have to.'

But no matter what they did, they couldn't wake me. Because I wasn't asleep. I had left my body, and now had to wait until it was safe to return. If it would ever be safe for me now that Dr Wood had discovered my secret.

Well, part of it. She didn't know my spirit was no longer

193

in my body.

'Get Anthony,' she said to the orderly. 'He can explain how he got it so wrong and tell me how to wake her up.'

Aware Anthony would be able to hear me telepathically, I decided it was time to leave, even though I was worried about what they might do to my body while I was gone. No doubt I would be covered in bruises and sore for days just from what Dr Wood had already put me through.

How could Lachlan still be capable of walking and talking, exercising even, after several sessions of this?

As the orderly moved to a phone on the desk I headed out the door and made my way downstairs. I burst into Lachlan's room, gasping when I ran through his body. He'd been standing at the door, looking out the window.

He spun around, shivering as he scanned the room, concern in his eyes. 'Rose, was that you? Are you okay? I thought I heard you scream,' he said, tapping the side of his head. 'In here.'

'It was me,' I said, firing the words out. 'Dr Wood electrocuted me. I was screaming when I took astral form, and she heard me. She knows I have an ability. The graph showed her I did something. With my mind. They were trying to wake me, to get me to tell them what my ability was.'

I remembered how furious and yet excited Dr Wood had been by the discovery, and a shudder swept through my spirit. It was more important than ever that we escaped. If she hooked me up to that machine again, I would babble all my secrets for sure, ruining everything. But what could I do, cut off from my body?

I couldn't remain in the astral plane forever. Sooner or later I'd have to return to my physical body, and then Dr Wood would make me pay for deceiving her.

10

'You need to get out of here, find Belinda and let her know what's happening,' said Lachlan. 'Her cop boyfriend can help you.'

'I can't leave. My body is still strapped to that bed.' I wanted to though. I wanted to run away and never look back. To hide from my failure to do anything right. Father had been right. I was useless.

Ethereal tears slid down my cheeks, sparkling in the air around me.

Lachlan sucked in a breath. 'You're not useless.'

Stifling a sob, I shook my head. 'I can't even pick up a ball. How am I supposed to find someone I've never met before?'

Lachlan stiffened. 'Damn it, Rose. I'm not asking. I'm telling. Go now, before you get drawn back to your body and ruin everything for both of us.'

When I let out another sob his expression softened. 'Please, you have to go. If you stay they will start you on the happy juice, make you do things to hurt others. You'll end up like me, burned out and locked in the basement, haunted by what you've been made to do. You have to go, to stop that happening to you and the others upstairs.'

Every word he said struck a chord with the fear building inside of me. But even more, the pain threaded through his words had my tears flowing anew. He'd been through so much, had risen above the darkness ensnaring him to find the strength to help Belinda. And then paid the price for betraying

Dr Frankel.

Smiling through my tears, I said, 'I thought you didn't care about the others. All you care about is getting out of here, that's what you said.'

'I don't care. But Belinda's boyfriend hates me. He wouldn't lift a finger to help me, but he'll do everything he can to save you and the others trapped here.'

I was glad he couldn't see me smile. Everything he said and did showed he was more concerned about me and the other prisoners than he wanted to let on. But I still had no idea how to find Belinda or her boyfriend.

'We don't even know where Belinda is. How am I supposed to find her?'

'I don't know. But you have to try, Rose.' His voice broke on my name, and he took a moment to regain his composure. 'I don't want Frankel to turn you into one of his weapons. Please, try to find Belinda and her cousin. They're the only ones who can help you now.'

'Okay, I'll try.'

I said goodbye to Lachlan, not sure how I could make good on my promise. As I floated upstairs to the ground floor I considered the problems I would have to overcome. Find a way to Easton and search the entire town until I found Grace and hope she could lead me to the others. With luck I would be able to communicate with Liam, as I did with Lachlan. But what if I found them and it didn't work?

No, I had to stop thinking like that.

I would find them, and I would find a way to communicate with them.

The carpark out front of the building was filled with cars, as well as a couple of white vans, but none of them had logos on the side. It seemed BioTech was keeping a low profile. I followed a long winding driveway bordered by trees, and eventually came to a gate, with a road running past the entrance.

Now I had to make a choice on which way to go.

I floated into the middle of the road, just above the traffic that zoomed past on either side of me. I saw no sign of habitation in either direction, no clue pointing to Easton. But I had promised Lachlan I would find the others.

I closed my eyes, hovering in mid-air, thinking about Grace and Liam as I had last seen them, waiting for my body to be pulled from the rubble.

I felt a tug deep within my astral form and tensed, sure I was about to be pulled back to my physical body. But the tug seemed to be coming from the left of me.

Was it a sign?

To test my theory, I thought about Lachlan, picturing him as he'd done push-ups, muscles working in his back, a layer of sweat covering his naked skin.

This time the tug was stronger, leading back toward the building he was trapped in.

Mind made up, I turned to the left and focused once more on Grace and Liam.

I picked up speed as I went, the tug strengthening with every kilometre I travelled.

Soon it was as if I was flying, and despite the reason for my haste it felt wonderful to be streaking through the air, unseen by those below me, my ethereal form dancing in the wind and hair pushed back from my face.

Eventually I reached Easton and my speed began to slow as I flew over the tops of buildings and streets. I soon came to a halt in front of a large two-storey house. The tug that had brought me here faded as I slipped through the front door and blinked to accustom my eyes to the dimness after being outside in the sun.

197

I saw a group of people seated in a large lounge room, many of them holding coffee cups. I recognised the guy who had healed me, sitting next to a girl who looked like Andie but didn't feel like her. I couldn't explain how I knew it wasn't her, it just felt right to say she was Angel, Andie's twin sister.

I couldn't see Andie, but I heard her voice coming from another room, along with others. But the fact I'd found them wasn't the reason for the wide smile that curved my face.

Sitting opposite Angel and the guy with black hair were Grace and Liam. Grace had tears in her eyes as she shook her head.

'There's still no sign of Rose. We need to find her.'

'Grace, I'm here,' I said, even if technically only part of me was present.

Liam's head spun to face me. 'Did you hear that?' He looked at the others in the room. 'I thought I heard Rose call out to Grace.'

Grace shook her head. 'I didn't hear anything.'

'I did,' said the guy who had healed me, while Angel nodded.

'We heard it too,' said Andie as she entered the room with a girl with red hair at her heels. Behind them were the young men Father had chosen to be Liam's attendants, Daniel and Nick, but they looked as confused as Grace did.

"She said she was here,' said Liam, scanning the room and of course not seeing me.

'It's me, Rose,' I said. 'But I'm not really here. My spirit is, but my body is somewhere else.'

Liam's face paled. 'You're dead?'

Grace gasped and clutched his arm. 'You're talking to her ghost?'

'I'm not dead,' I hastened to say. At least, I hoped my body was still alive back at the estate. I pushed fear for my welfare aside and focused on the problem at hand. 'I'm in astral form. I travelled from the place where we're being held to find you.'

'We? You mean the other missing members of the Order are there as well?' Liam asked.

'Yes, and a guy called Lachlan Dales is there too.'

I heard another gasp, this time coming from behind me and I turned to find a girl with dark hair standing in the doorway. 'Is Lachlan okay?'

Her voice throbbed with concern, and a twinge of jealousy surged through me. Who was she, and how did she know Lachlan?'

'He's fine,' I said, voice less jubilant now. 'At least he was last time I spoke to him.'

'I don't understand,' said Grace. 'I thought Rose couldn't communicate mentally.' She looked around the room.

'Tell Grace I can only use telepathy when I'm in astral form. It doesn't work otherwise,' I said.

'How did you figure out you could astral project?' Liam asked.

'It was back at the church, when I was trapped under the rubble.' I explained the first time I'd had an out of body experience, and then learning how to do it again after I woke up to find myself at the mercy of BioTech.

Liam relayed my words to Grace and the others who couldn't hear me.

'BioTech? I've never heard of that company,' said Nick. 'Anyone else have any idea what she's talking about?'

They all shook their heads.

'It's run by Dr Frankel. He's using people with psychic abilities to do bad things.'

Before I could tell them what had happened to Marie, everyone in the room began talking at once.

A new voice chimed in, Angel's, her hands flashing in sign language as she asked everyone to be quiet so I could continue with my story.

Conscious of how long I had been away from my body, I kept it short, earning more gasps when I told about Lachlan, Marie and me being tortured by Dr Wood and that we were being held at what used to be the Wood Estate.

'That's impossible. She's supposed to be locked in a mental institution,' said Celeste, looking even more worried than the others.

'Dr Frankel said something about arranging for her to be released. She's in charge of assessing the abilities of everyone they captured,' I said. 'Lachlan said I had to find Belinda, so her boyfriend could get the police involved in our rescue. They have dozens of armed guards, and people brainwashed to use their abilities for them.'

The girl who had asked after Lachlan stepped forward, a phone held to her ear. 'I'm Belinda. I'm calling Scott now. Now we know where Lachlan and the others are, the taskforce he works for will be able to help us get you and the others out of there.'

I hoped she was right. I also hoped it wouldn't take long. While I felt no hunger or thirst, or any other form of discomfort while in astral form, my body would be suffering the effects if I was away too much longer. There was no telling what Dr Wood was doing to me right now; what condition my body was in. But I couldn't risk going back yet.

When Belinda's boyfriend arrived, he was not alone. A stunning young woman with black hair and brown eyes walked in along with an older man with close cropped brown hair and an intense gaze as he scanned the room. I was sure he didn't miss much and figured he had to be someone important even before Scott introduced him as the leader of the taskforce he worked for, Detective Sam Lockwood.

But it was the young woman, Tyler Morgan, who intrigued me more. She was staring straight at me, almost as if she saw me, while the others were introduced to the detective.

She stepped closer, frowning as she lifted a hand, almost as though she wanted to touch me. Before her hand could come into contact with my ethereal form her eyes widened, and she stepped back.

'You're not dead,' she said.

'You can see me?'

'Of course I can see you.' Tyler scanned the room and seemed to take in the stunned expressions of the others. 'I'm guessing none of you can see the girl with the curly hair floating in the middle of the room?'

'We can hear her,' said Liam. 'Well, some of us can.' He gave Grace a hug before turning back to Tyler. 'But that's it. We can't see her.'

'Hmmm.' Tyler turned back to look at me. 'I've heard there are those among the living who can access the astral plane while in a higher state of consciousness. I usually only encounter dead souls, or those who can physically enter the astral plane.'

'Dead souls?' I frowned, shaking off the thought to focus on what else she had said. 'You said some people can enter the astral plane physically. I didn't think that was possible. I mean, an out of body experience is meant to be, well, out of body.'

'There are … people among us who have the ability to move through the different planes.'

I shook my head, unable to comprehend how someone could physically be in the astral plane. I couldn't even manage to touch a stupid ball.

Then Tyler did something, moved, and suddenly she was

right there beside me. It was not like before. Now I felt energy rippling through her body and saw a silvery light much brighter than the one given off by my astral form.

The others in the room gasped and cried out.

'Where did she go?' Nick waved a hand in the air where Tyler had been moments before.

'Relax, people,' said Detective Lockwood, showing no sign of surprise. 'Tyler is just visiting your friend in the astral plane. She'll be back soon.'

'Can she bring Rose back with her?' Grace asked.

Tyler slipped back into the physical plane, side-stepping Nick, and answered, 'I'm afraid not. Her body isn't here for her to enter, so pulling her spirit out of the astral plane would be dangerous.' She grimaced, and I guessed there was a lot she'd left unsaid. I had more important things to worry about.

'Can you teach me how to get into the astral plane the way you just did?' It was clear she had vanished from the sight of everyone, even though I could still see her. If she could teach me how to do the same thing then I would be able to return to the estate and free Lachlan from his room.

'I'm afraid it is something you need to be born with,' said Tyler.

The momentary hope died away. Still, 'What about teaching me how to touch something without my fingers passing through it?'

'In time, perhaps I could teach you that, but from what Sam told me on the way here we don't have that long. We need to stop BioTech using any more of your friends as weapons.'

'Which isn't going to be easy,' said Detective Lockwood. 'They're on a list of companies we are not supposed to get involved with.'

'What do you mean?' Grace asked.

'They're a government contractor, and someone high up has given them security clearance and immunity to stop the police from investigating or curtailing their actions.'

'But that's crazy,' Daniel burst out.

'Tell me about it.' Detective Lockwood's voice was grim. 'I've been working for weeks to get the order overturned, but the official on my side died unexpectedly, drowning in his bath last night.'

Oh no.

It all fell into place.

Dr Frankel had worked fast to remove a threat to his company, using Marie to do it.

With powerful members of the government backing BioTech, it would make it impossible for us to free Lachlan and the others, and as soon as I returned to my physical body I would be trapped there for good as well.

11

'Rose, I need you to—'

The faint cry echoed through my head before cutting off abruptly.

'Lachlan.' I spun in the air, searching for him.

Belinda gasped. 'I heard him too,' she said. 'He's in trouble.'

'I have to go back. I have to help him,' I said. Lachlan's voice had been filled with pain. They had to be torturing him again.

'I'll come with you,' said Tyler, moving over to sit on the couch.

'Tyler, are you sure about this?' Detective Lockwood moved to her side and placed a hand on her shoulder, concern brimming in his eyes.

'From what Rose has told us, BioTech don't know about astral projection. I can infiltrate the facility and see what's happening while she helps this Lachlan. We need to find something we can use to get them shut down. The government can't know they're using psychics to commit murder.'

'I wouldn't be too sure of that,' said Detective Lockwood, eyes narrowed.

'Should Rose stay here, until her physical body is safe?' Scott asked.

'Lachlan is in trouble,' said Belinda. 'She needs to go to him.'

'Lachlan's a criminal,' he said, a dark expression in his eyes.

Belinda took his hand. 'Dr Frankel made him do those things. It wasn't his fault.'

I remembered the haunted expression in Lachlan's eyes when he'd admitted he'd done bad things, that he wasn't a nice guy. What he'd been made to do was eating him up inside. Scott might not think he needed saving, but at least Belinda agreed with me, soothing some of the jealousy I'd felt at knowing they had some kind of connection.

'We need to go now,' I said to Tyler, watching on as she settled herself into a comfortable position and slipped out of her body.

Her astral form was beautiful, the silver light surrounding her almost blinding. I squinted, and gasped when I saw she even had silvery wings. I peered behind me, but there was nothing like that for me, though the way my astral form swirled in the air was almost like having wings.

She gave a light laugh. 'Sorry, that part is unique to me. Though I'm sure you have your own specialness,' she said, accurately reading my actions.

She said goodbye to the detective, running a gossamer hand down his cheek. Then she headed to the door. Once we'd passed through it she streaked off and I was hard pressed to keep up with her. She adjusted her speed to mine and gave me tips on how to improve my flight through the astral plane.

This time, I saw silvery balls of light hovering in the air around us, around her. She gave a sad smile any time one of them came close, but they darted away before she could reach out and touch them.

'Friends of yours?' I asked.

'You could say that,' she said.

It was hard for me to remember any landmarks from my journey to find Grace, but this time I focused on Lachlan, my sense of him growing stronger, tugging me in the direction we needed to go. We didn't slow down until we got to the estate and were halfway down the winding driveway at the front.

More armed guards patrolled the grounds than before, at least a dozen of them stationed in the newly constructed guard post at the gate as we'd come through.

We split up, Tyler going to gather information for the taskforce, while I followed the tug to Lachlan. It led me below ground, but as I floated toward the stairs it did not take me past the exit to the second level. He was on the floor in the room where I had been subjected to shock treatment by Dr Wood.

I was not surprised when the pull took me to the door. I stood on the other side mentally preparing myself for what I would find when I entered.

Lachlan gave an anguished cry, once again calling out my name. Only this time there was a warning in it. It sounded as though he was telling me to stay away, but more cries of agony followed. I couldn't stay away. I had to help him.

I burst through the door and gazed in horror at what I found.

My body was still strapped to the bed, while Lachlan was strapped to the one next to it.

From the looks of it he had been hooked up to the electric shock machine for some time, his body arched so all the tendons in his muscles stood out as he tugged on the straps holding him down. As I watched Dr Wood turned the machine off and he sagged back to the bed.

'Lachlan,' I cried out as I rushed to the side of his bed.

'Rose, get out of here. It's a trap.'

Lachlan's warning resonated inside my head, but it took me a moment to understand what he was saying.

The needle on the ECG whirred to life, indicating his mental spike.

As soon as she saw it, Dr Wood gave Anthony a delighted smile. 'Do it,' she said.

Anthony, who stood beside my bed, produced the Taser and placed it against my arm and flicked the switch.

A ripple went through my astral form as my physical body convulsed on the bed. I felt a sharp tug and no matter how much I resisted it pulled me closer to my body. I slammed into it and instantly tried to scream as the current from the Taser flowed through me. My scream was strangled by the gag in my mouth.

It seemed like forever before the current left my body and I lay limp, gasping for breath, muscles twitching in remembered pain.

When I could think again, I tried to turn my head sideways, to look at Lachlan, but the straps held me immobile.

'Nice of you to join us,' said Dr Wood as she leaned over me and grabbed my chin, giving it a painful twist. 'It seems you've been keeping secrets from us.'

I struggled to focus, still in pain from the shock treatment. I couldn't have responded to her even if I didn't have a gag in my mouth. But it seemed she didn't need me to talk. She turned to Anthony.

'Put her upstairs with the others, and make sure she is guarded at all times. When we're finished with Lachlan I can figure out what her ability is and how we can use it.'

I felt a sharp sting in my shoulder, and a familiar dizziness washed over me. I tried to pull my spirit out of my body, but something stopped me from taking astral form as Anthony unstrapped me from the bed and scooped me into his arms. He carried me to the door and I caught sight of Lachlan, an anguished expression in his eyes as he watched on. If he said anything to me, telepathically, I couldn't hear it.

The door closed, and I lost sight of Lachlan, giving in to

the sedative running through my veins, lying limp in Anthony's grasp as he entered the elevator and jostled me around so he could push the button for it to go up.

I didn't know what to do, how to get out of this predicament. If I couldn't slip into the astral plane I wouldn't be able to warn Tyler about what had happened.

Soon Anthony laid me down on a bed, perhaps the one I'd slept in my first night at the estate, and then left the room. I opened my eyes long enough to see that a guard stood inside the room, in front of the closed door, watching me, and then I closed them again to have another go at slipping into the astral plane.

A slap on my face had me gasping, eyes flying open to find the guard leaning over me.

'Stay awake,' he said.

I rubbed my cheek and glared at him as he returned to his post near the door. He made no sign that he was disturbed by my reaction.

The sedative in my veins was enough to make me drowsy, but not the knockout drug to make me sleep. As I thought about it, I realised this made sense. Somehow, they knew I would be able to take astral form if drugged or unconscious. They wanted me awake, to make sure I was still there in spirit as well as in body.

I had to come up with a way of letting my spirit escape that didn't let them know it was happening.

I pushed myself into a sitting position, leaning back against the bedhead, and tried to shift myself into the astral plane with my eyes open so the guard wouldn't know what I was doing. But before I could do anything he gave a cry, clutching his chest, face white as he slumped sideways, landing in a heap on the floor.

I jumped off the bed and ran over to him, checking his

pulse.

'It's okay. He's alive.'

Tyler's voice came from right beside me, making me jump.

'What? How can I hear you? I'm not in astral form.'

'I can't communicate telepathically,' she said. 'I'm not psychic. But we don't have time for me to explain. I need to return to Sam and the others, to tell them what's going on. Are you going to be okay while I'm gone?'

I nodded, feeling strange talking to someone I couldn't see. Was it that way for Lachlan, when we talked while I was in astral form?

'The guard will be unconscious for a while, and I'll unlock the door for you, so you can find somewhere to hide while you wait for the cavalry to arrive. I'll be back as soon as I can.'

I felt a slight wind push against me and imagined Tyler unfurling her silver wings. Seconds later the door unlocked and swung open. I poked my head out the door, checking the hallway was empty before I left the dubious safety of my room. I closed the door behind me and locked it, hoping it would be a while before anyone noticed the guard was unconscious or that I was free.

Of course, they'd discover I'd escaped my room soon enough if I was spotted.

'Good luck.' Tyler's whisper came from beside me, and another gush of air, this one stronger than before. Then came silence.

I was on my own, but I had no intention of finding somewhere to hide as Tyler had suggested. For the first time since I'd got here I was unaccompanied by a guard or orderly while in physical form. I had to make the most of it, find a way to get Lachlan out of the treatment room. For all I knew he was still strapped to the bed and being tortured by Dr Wood.

I kept my back straight and walked determinedly down the hall, hoping that if I did encounter someone they would think I was meant to be there.

There was no one in sight, and when I glanced at the clock on the wall above the elevator I saw it was lunchtime. Presumably everyone was in the dining hall.

I pushed the button to take me to the lower level but nothing happened. Then I remembered the guard had used a key when I'd first been taken down there.

I cursed, knowing I wouldn't be able to get to Lachlan that way. I pushed the button for the ground floor. That worked, so I rode down and then left the elevator to make my way to the emergency stairwell. My confidence that I could free Lachlan plummeted when the code the guard had used to unlock the door to my room did not work on the keypad to this door. I couldn't go any farther.

Begrudging the time it took, I headed for the offices behind the common room, making my way to Dr Wood's room. The door was unlocked, and I listened for a moment before twisting the handle and slipping inside.

Then I began to search for a key, a different code, something I could use to get to Lachlan.

If she had a key, it wasn't in any of the desk drawers. Neither was there a convenient titled piece of paper stating the code to any of the keypads locking the emergency exits.

I went to leave her room, intending to try one of the other offices to see if I had better luck, but the sound of heavy footsteps in the hall outside the room brought me to a halt.

I opened the door just enough to peer through the crack. It was too soon for Tyler to have returned to her physical body and organised a rescue. I wasn't even sure a rescue would be

210

happening if the detective was not able to find a way around the order to stay away from BioTech.

Guards ran down the hallway, guns in their hands, faces grim.

Anthony was with them, and he paused in the middle of the hall, metres away from the door to Dr Wood's office.

'She can't have got far,' he said into a hand-held radio. 'Her ability leaves her body unprotected. She'll be holed up in a cupboard somewhere.'

So much for hoping it would take them a while to discover the unconscious guard. Anthony was right. I wouldn't be able to leave my body lying just anywhere. If I was in the astral plane all he would need to do was to shock me to get me to return to my body, the way he had done before.

I couldn't stay where I was either. Once they ran out of cupboards to search, the offices would surely be next. It became even more imperative that I found a way to get below ground. They would never expect me to hide my physical body there.

I was still left with the same problem. I didn't know the code for the emergency exit and I didn't have a key to work the elevator.

Out of options, I closed the door to Dr Wood's office and locked it, leaning up against it as I tried to think my way through my dilemma.

12

With no other option presenting itself, I left Dr Wood's office. I would continue to search as best I could, hoping I would find something to help us before I was discovered, or the promised rescue arrived.

After checking three more offices I still had nothing to show for it. Then, in the fourth office, I found something that offered a glimmer of hope.

A lab coat was slung over the back of a chair, and a handbag left sitting on the desk.

The office was clearly used by a woman, one who was around my size. The lab coat fitted perfectly when I slid it on. With it buttoned up at the front, I hoped no one would realise I wore the exercise clothes the nurse had given me that morning.

Rummaging through the handbag, I found a set of keys, one of them the electronic key for a car. I slipped the keys in a pocket of the coat, hoping one of them would be for the elevator. I also found a hair tie and a set of sunglasses. I quickly scraped my hair back into a tight ponytail and then placed the glasses on top of my head, using the arms to hold back any escaping curls. With a small prayer that this was enough of a disguise, I left the office and headed for the elevator.

The door opened and an orderly and a nurse stepped out. They were ones I hadn't seen before, and I kept my face averted as they exited the elevator. The two of them seemed engrossed in their conversation and took little notice of me as

I slipped past them into the elevator.

Once the doors closed, I grabbed out the keys and tried to match one with the keyhole beside the buttons for the sub levels.

The third key I tried fitted and I pushed down on a surge of excitement as I pressed the button for L2.

When the doors opened I waited for a moment, listening for signs there was anyone about. When I couldn't hear anything, I left the elevator and made my way to the door of the treatment room. I still heard nothing, but with the door closed it was impossible to tell if anyone was inside.

Only one way to find out.

I opened the door and peered in.

The lights were off, and from what I saw from the doorway both beds were empty. Not sure if I should feel relieved or anxious, I headed back to the elevator and selected L3.

I hoped the empty room on level two meant Lachlan had been returned to his room. But what if that wasn't the case? What if something had happened to him while I'd been trying to figure out a way to get down here? For all I knew he could have been taken upstairs as I had been.

Again, there was only one way to find out.

I was ready when the elevator doors slid open, but not prepared for what I found.

Lachlan stood in front of me, a rifle in his hands, blood dribbling from a gash on his forehead. Two guards were sprawled on the floor behind him, seemingly unconscious.

The rifle was pointed at me but when I called out his name shock replaced the grim determination in his eyes and he lowered the weapon.

'Rose, you're okay.'

He stepped forward and wrapped his free arm around me,

pulling me close. Then he pressed his face into my hair, which muffled his voice.

'Thank God. I was so worried about you.'

'Me too,' I said. 'Worried about you, I mean. I was coming to rescue you.'

He relaxed his grip but didn't let go as he leaned back and smiled down at me. 'You were going to rescue me, huh?'

'Yes. We need to get out of here right away. Something big is going to happen.'

He ushered me back into the elevator and as it rode to the ground floor I gave him a quick recount of what had happened while I'd been away.

Beside me, Lachlan stiffened when I mentioned Detective Lockwood and the taskforce. 'So, the police are on their way here,' he said in a sombre voice.

'Why don't you sound as if you think that is a good thing?' I pulled away and stared at him. 'You sent me to get help.'

'I know what I asked you to do,' he said with a grimace. 'But I guess I didn't think about the consequences if you succeeded. I told you before, I've done bad things. Things that will get me arrested. If your friends really are on the way here with the police, I'll just be replacing one jail cell with another.'

'Dr Frankel made you do those bad things. It wasn't your fault.'

'The police won't care about that. Particularly Scott Carlton. He's got no reason to think kindly of me, not after what I did to Belinda.'

I remembered Scott's expression and what he'd said back at Angel's house. But Belinda had stood up for Lachlan. Surely between us we could make Scott and Detective Lockwood see that Lachlan shouldn't be punished for what Dr

Frankel had made him do.

But that was a problem to worry about at another time.

The elevator had arrived at the ground floor and we still hadn't come up with a plan to get us out of there. With the number of guards roaming all over the place, not to mention all the staff and how they could make the prisoners use their abilities on us, it was not going to be easy. Not that any number of guards or other obstacles would stop us trying our best to escape.

We stepped out of the elevator, Lachlan a little ahead of me with his weapon ready. Prisoners and guards were scattered around the common room. Before any of them could register our arrival, the ground rumbled beneath us. At first it was just a slight rumble, shaking the floor, but then it got bigger, fast.

Soon it was hard to remain standing as cracks appeared in the walls.

Shouts of alarm sounded throughout the building as prisoners, nurses and orderlies panicked. Lachlan and I took advantage of the confusion, making for the hall that led to the front reception. A nurse was already there, struggling to stay upright as she punched in the code that opened the door. A siren began to wail as a steady stream of people entered the hallway behind us. Lachlan tucked his rifle inside his lab coat, concealing it as we followed the nurse out into the reception area, making straight for the front doors.

People screamed as the glass wall exploded, and I covered my head with my arm as shards rained down on us. But I didn't stop and neither did Lachlan. Around us some of the staff were calling out instructions, telling everyone where to meet outside. With so many panicked people it was hard for them to keep track of who was a prisoner and who worked there.

As soon as we were outside, Lachlan and I ran for the driveway, intending to lose ourselves in the trees.

As more and more people streamed from the building behind us, we increased our speed, needing to get to cover before people figured out we were heading in the wrong direction.

Shouts came from behind us, and the sound of a gunshot cut through the din. Dirt puffed up to my left and I veered right, only to have another shot hit the ground a metre away from me. I darted a look behind me and found four guards were chasing us.

'Stop right now or I will shoot you.'

The shout chilled my blood, but I couldn't stop, not with Lachlan still dragging me along behind him. If we could just get to the trees, I was sure we would be safe.

Head down, I tried to increase my speed, lungs hurting as I struggled to gasp in air.

More shots rang out, a sharp pain erupting in my left calf. I stumbled, crying out as I crashed to the ground, my hand wrenched out of Lachlan's by the force of my fall. I hit hard, what little air I had in my lungs pushed out by the impact with the packed dirt in front of the tree line. I rolled onto my side, gasping in air as I clutched my calf. Blood soaked through my fingers, pain making me dizzy as I tried to stem the flow.

Lachlan threw himself to his knees beside me, face contorted with anger as he raised his rifle and aimed it at the advancing guards. A shot rang out and he reeled, dropping the rifle to clutch at his shoulder.

The guards reached us, standing in a line, weapons pointed at us. One of them moved in and scooped up Lachlan's rifle.

It was over. Our escape attempt failed before it had even properly begun.

Still clutching my calf, I wriggled over to Lachlan's side, leaning against him as we waited.

He gave a sigh. 'I'm sorry, Rose. I thought I could protect you.'

'It's okay. We'll be okay,' I said, trying to ignore the screaming in my calf and the steady flow of blood that was leaking through my fingers to pool on the ground.

Lachlan looked over at me, fear and despair etched on his face. He shook his head. But before he could say anything more a wall of fire sprang up between the guards and us, heat blazing from it.

The guards shouted in surprise as they moved back, hands up to shield their faces.

One of them fired through the flames at us, but the bullet stopped in mid-air even as a bolt of lightning speared the ground in front of him.

Hands grasped my shoulders and I twisted around, sure I was about to face a new threat, sagging in relief when I met Ethan's eyes.

'We've been shot,' I said, grateful the promised rescue had arrived.

Ethan gave a nod as he crouched beside me and placed both hands on my injured leg. I felt a wave of warmth flood through my body as the agony in my calf subsided. Then he moved over to take care of Lachlan.

Wiping bloody hands on my pants, I looked behind us and smiled at the sight of Angel, Andie and Celeste lined up, holding hands, facing the way we had come.

We were finally safe.

Not ready to trust my legs to hold me up, I stayed sitting on the ground as I watched Lachlan be healed. He blinked in amazement as Ethan worked the bullet out and then healed the wound it had left.

217

Once Ethan was finished, Lachlan put a hand up to his head and said, 'My ability. You healed it.'

Happiness filled me to see the wondrous smile on his face. I leaned over and gave his leg a quick squeeze as I turned back to see what was happening in front of the building.

Belinda, Liam and Grace stood just behind Angel and the others, watching.

Ethan got up and moved to take Angel's free hand and the ground began to rumble even louder than before.

'The building is empty,' said Celeste. 'Everyone is clear.'

'Let's trash this sucker,' said Andie, exultation in her voice.

Mouth gaping open I stared as the building was destroyed. Fire, lightning and earthquakes tore it apart until all that was left was smouldering rubble.

Then I cowered back when Dr Frankel and Dr Wood ran toward us, a host of guards at their back, all of them with grim expressions. Anthony was with them, along with more former members of the Order, those with stronger abilities than the others who had been kidnapped. It was clear they had been ordered to subdue us.

I turned to see where Angel and the others were, hoping they had enough energy left to dispel this new threat. I knew how much it must have taken for them to have levelled the place where they had been imprisoned and tortured by Dr Wood.

My fear was justified when I saw their shoulders slumping.

They had no energy left to stop Frankel and his goons. Worse, they were vulnerable. Dr Frankel had been after them all along, and this failed escape attempt had delivered them to him. BioTech would be able to rise from the ashes, and we would be even worse off than we had been before.

No, I would not let that happen. I would not let him and Dr Wood destroy any more lives, or turn people like Marie into weapons.

Rage filled me, and I let instinct take over.

My physical body fell to the ground as I took astral form, screaming my defiance.

Dr Frankel and Dr Wood dropped to the ground, hands over their ears as my scream reverberated in the air around us. The guards fell too, along with Anthony and the others. Soon every single person who had been in front of me was on the ground, cowering as my scream battered their senses.

The sound of my scream died away, and as soon as it did our enemies struggled back to their feet and moved toward us once more.

It wasn't enough. I'd done everything I could, but it wasn't enough.

Then Liam stepped forward.

'Stop,' he called out in a commanding tone, and the group surging toward us froze.

Of course. Liam had the power to compel those without an ability to obey him. Only Anthony and the other psychics were unaffected, but from the looks on their faces they realised they were on the losing side.

When Liam finished issuing his commands, he and Anthony shared what appeared to be a silent conversation. Anthony was the first to turn away, weaving through the crowd of people and disappearing with the other psychics. The guards were the next to leave, brows furrowed as they looked at the weapons they had discarded at Liam's command, as if unsure what to do now they had been disarmed and ordered to find more suitable employment. Dr Wood was the one who showed the most change as she clung to Dr Frankel's arms.

'We need a car, to take us to Easton,' she said, and Frankel nodded in response.

Liam had ordered them to present themselves to the nearest police station to turn themselves in and confess everything they had done on behalf of BioTech.

Astral form wilted, I returned to my body.

As soon as I sat up, Grace ran forward and clasped my hand. 'I'm so glad you're okay. I was afraid we wouldn't get here in time,' she said, surprising me with a quick hug.

I returned her hug and smiled over at Lachlan.

He wore a scowl as he got to his feet and stared at Belinda.

'Took you long enough,' he said.

Belinda gave a light laugh and my stomach knotted when she scooted forward to kiss him on the cheek. 'You're welcome,' she said, 'and thank you for everything you did for me.'

His scowl lightened somewhat as he scanned the area behind us. 'So, where's the cop boyfriend? I was sure he'd be here, itching to arrest me.'

Belinda's expression darkened. 'He was forbidden to get involved. All of the members of the taskforce were. BioTech was off limits as far as their superiors were concerned.'

Lachlan gave her a crooked smile. 'Didn't stop you lot, though.'

'We're civilians,' said Andie. 'They don't get to tell us what we can and can't do.'

She and the others shared smiles, but the knot had not left my stomach. Lachlan was still a wanted man. As soon as we left here he would be arrested for sure.

I couldn't let that happen. Not until we'd found a way to show the police he wasn't to blame for what BioTech and Dr

Frankel had made him do.

I needed to get him away from here, hide him until after Dr Frankel and Dr Wood had been to the police and their confessions showed who was really to blame.

I moved to his side and grabbed his hand, pulling him away from the others slightly. In a low voice, I explained my plan.

'It's only going to delay the inevitable,' he said, voice bleak.

'Please, Lachlan. Just give it a few days, and then we'll go to the police. Everything should be cleared up by then.'

He wore a dubious expression, but he didn't protest as we waited for the others to be distracted by the mass of people milling in front of the ruined building to sneak off through the crowd.

After pressing the electronic key in my pocket, we found the car it belonged to and were soon speeding away from the estate.

I tensed as we passed a line of police cars heading the way we had come, but they paid no attention to us. Nor did the fire engines and ambulances that followed in their wake.

I didn't feel happy about sneaking away without saying goodbye to Grace and Liam, but I would explain everything when it was safe to do so.

I only hoped they would understand when they heard the truth.

13

I pushed Lachlan behind me as I stared at the people milling in the area in front of the ruined church. Much of the rubble had been cleared away and they continued to work to remove the rest.

One of them turned around and spotted us. 'Rose,' she said, a smile wreathing her face. The smile quickly faded when she took a good look at Lachlan and me in our bloodstained clothes.

'Oh my God, are you two okay?'

'We're fine. We've been healed,' I said, not recognising her for a moment. Then I looked past the streak of dirt coating one side of her face. 'Bernice?'

She gave a nod. 'We were so worried about you, after the police said you'd gone missing. I'm so glad to see you're okay. I hope you don't mind us staying here. We've tried to be useful.'

I looked at the others, who had stopped their labours to stand around us. No longer dressed in white, all with streaks of dirt, I hardly recognised them as Father's followers.

I scanned their faces, noting the absence of any of his inner circle, and breathed a sigh of relief. But I still didn't understand why they were here, working to clear away the remains of the church.

'We didn't have anywhere else to go,' said Bernice, her simple statement accompanied by a shrug. 'So once the police gave clearance, we moved back in. No one is staying in your house, if that's what worries you.'

I hadn't given it a thought, but I left them to their work and led Lachlan over to the wooden house Father had insisted be the first building erected when we'd moved from the old motel we'd lived in to the compound.

Lachlan had kept silent during my exchange with the former members of the Order, and seemed content to let me take the lead as we walked over to my old home.

I stepped inside and scanned the contents. Nothing appeared to have been changed. Everything looking exactly as it had when I had last been in here, before Father insisted I move to the attendants' quarters across from Liam and Grace's room.

Yet, the place felt totally different, larger and brighter than I remembered it.

It took me a moment to work out what the difference was.

Father was not here; his overwhelming presence wasn't beating me down with rules of silence and obedience. I was free of him. Free to make my own life.

I turned to Lachlan and took his hands. 'We can stay here.'

He frowned. 'Won't that lot out there dob us in to the police?'

'Why would they? They have no reason to know you are a wanted man.

'Not that it matters. Now you have somewhere safe to stay, I can turn myself in.'

'Lachlan, no. You can't go to the police yet.'

He tugged on my hands, pulling me closer and then letting go to wrap his arms around me.

'It has to be this way. I did terrible things. I have to pay for that. I won't put you or the others in danger, get you in trouble, because of what I did.'

'It wasn't your fault. Dr Frankel made you do those

223

things. He used drugs to control you. You had no choice but to do what he wanted.'

He released me and stepped back, hands going to the pockets of his jeans.

'I had a choice, back when I first figured out what he was up to. I could have walked away, gone to the hospital, the police, someone, and asked for help. But I didn't. That's on me. I have to turn myself in.'

'I'm glad to hear you say that.'

I turned at the sound of a deep voice, stomach clenching at the sight of Detective Lockwood, his determined gaze fixed on Lachlan.

I pulled Lachlan back and then stepped in front of him.

'You're not taking him,' I said, shaking my head.

'Rose, it's okay. Detective Lockwood won't hurt Lachlan.'

My heart raced at the sound of Grace's voice. I heard the murmur of more voices outside. Liam, Andie, and many others. They could help us. They could stop the detective from arresting Lachlan.

'Why don't we take this outside where we have more room?' said the detective, scanning the small living space.

'How did you find us?' asked Lachlan as soon as we stepped outside.

'Sorry, that was my fault. But I did it for you.'

Lachlan's eyes widened. 'Belinda.'

She stood beside Grace, long dark hair pulled back in a ponytail. Scott Carlton was on the other side of her, glaring at Lachlan.

Belinda turned to him, placing a hand on his arm. 'I know you want Lachlan to be punished for what he did, but if it wasn't for him, I might not be here now. He helped me escape from Dr Frankel. I'm hoping together we can find a way to keep him out of jail.'

'You want him to go free, after he helped Dr Frankel kidnap you?' said Scott, his glare softening as he faced Belinda.

'I'm not asking you to forgive him. But he saved me, and I do think he deserves a second chance,' she said, voice throaty with emotion.

Lachlan shook his head. 'You saved yourself. I didn't do anything. You would have found a way to get free with or without my help.'

I saw surprise in Scott's eyes at Lachlan's words. 'You're right. Belinda would never have given up.'

Belinda's brow creased as she glanced at Lachlan. 'If you hadn't shown me the way to the road, I would never have escaped. He would have taken my eyes. What you did... I can never thank you enough.'

'Yet you led the police here?' Lachlan's voice was even, showing no sign of anger.

'To find a compromise, one that doesn't end with you locked up for the rest of your life.'

Lachlan shook his head. 'A compromise isn't going to cut it.'

I held my breath when he gave me a crooked smile before turning to the detective and holding out his hands. 'I'm ready to go.'

'No.' I lunged in front of him, blocking him with my body. 'You can't arrest him.'

'Rose, it's okay. I have to go with the detective. I broke the law. Several times. I have to pay for that.'

I turned and placed my hands on his chest, looking up into his eyes. 'That wasn't you. That was Dr Frankel. He made you do it. You had no choice.'

Then I faced the detective again. 'Don't you see? To

blame Lachlan for doing what he had to do to survive; it's like blaming someone for breathing. He's finally free, able to make choices for himself, and all that goes away if you arrest him.'

'I'm afraid the law doesn't work like that. He has to go before a judge, and have his story heard,' said the detective.

'You do that and every one of us will be put back in the spotlight,' said Belinda. 'You saw what happened when news of my visions leaked to the press. No matter how hard you try to keep things quiet, they'll find out about Lachlan and what he can do, and then we'll all be in danger again.' She waved a hand toward Grace, Liam, Andie and the others. 'Wouldn't it be better to keep all this a secret? This place could be a valuable resource for fighting crime.'

'She's right,' I said. 'Everyone here can help you.'

Detective Lockwood's brow creased. 'They were planning on taking over the country. Not exactly the sort of allies I want.'

I shook my head. 'The ones who believed my father have gone. The ones left here didn't join the Order because they thought themselves to be superior. They came here because they had nowhere else to go. They'd been ostracised for who they are and what they can do. This is the only place they feel safe, and where they can be themselves. They will help you, and we can help them.'

'You know, it's not a bad idea,' said Scott. 'You know how much help Belinda's visions have been, and the others can do amazing things as well. We could use their help on some of the more specialised cases we encounter.'

Detective Lockwood rubbed his chin. 'We have Tyler.'

'She's awesome, but she can't be everywhere at once. And she can't create earthquakes, lighting or fireballs like this lot can.'

226

'Look, I get that some of the people here could be useful. But Lachlan Dales is a fugitive. We have to take him in. At the very least, we need to know what he knows about the clients Frankel had lined up.'

'Confine him to the compound until he tells us everything he knows, and we can be sure he's keeping on the right track,' said Scott, earning himself a grateful smile from Belinda.

I held my breath as I waited for the detective to answer.

Finally, he said, 'Fair enough, but it's your job to watch this compound.'

Then he turned his steady gaze on Lachlan. 'You put one foot wrong and I'll have you behind bars so fast you won't have time to blink, you got me?'

Lachlan gave him a solemn nod. 'You won't regret this, sir. I will not let you and Rose down.'

The detective left, and I turned to Lachlan, wrapping my arms around his waist and leaning in to lay my head on his chest as the former members of the Order came over to join us.

It wouldn't be easy, but in time this compound would become a haven for those people who had a psychic ability. I'd find Marie and the others BioTech had abused. Here we would teach those who wanted to learn how to control their powers and instil in them a code of practice that would make sure no one got any ideas that went against the tenets of the new Order of the Arcane.

And it would all happen with Lachlan at my side.

I turned my head and looked to where Andie, Angel, Celeste, Belinda and Grace stood, the remarkable young men who supported them at their sides, marvelling about how much everything had changed since I'd met them.

Being different no longer meant being alone.

Together we would shape the future into one that allowed

for the impossible to become reality.

ACKNOWLEDGEMENTS

It is hard to believe I have come to the end of the Arcane Awakenings Series. When I first wrote Angel Fire, I never imagined it would become the first in a series of six novellas. That would never have happened if it hadn't been for people wanting to know what was going to happen next for Andie and Angel. So, thank you to Mum and Danni, who were the two loudest voices asking for more. Their enthusiasm for my stories is incredible and makes me proud to be an author.

Thank you also to Donna, Jennifer and Jael, my cheer squad in all things writerly. To my family, thanks for sticking with me when I hide out in my writing cave, and for understanding when book stuff has turned my brain to mush.

Special thanks to Mariah Sinclair for the amazing covers she created for the Arcane Awakenings Series, and to Sally Odgers for helping to make my words shine. Sue-Ellen Pashley and DD Line are the best beta readers an author could have. These two wonderful ladies are always ready to read my stories and to catch any typos or plot holes. This series would not be published without their help.

Finally, thanks to the readers who have taken a chance on a new author. I hope you enjoy the last installment in the Arcane Awakenings series. If you would like to read more stories set in Easton, then check out my Reaper Series.

ABOUT THE AUTHOR

Shelley Russell Nolan is an avid reader who began writing her own stories at sixteen. Her first completed manuscript featured brain eating aliens and a butt kicking teenage heroine. Since then she has spent her time creating fantasy worlds where death is only the beginning and even freaks can fall in love.

The first two books in her debut adult urban fantasy series, *Lost Reaper* and *Winged Reaper*, were published by Atlas Productions in 2016, with *Silver Reaper* published in 2017 to complete the series. Odyssey Books will be publishing the first book in a new post-apocalyptic series in December 2018.

Born in New Zealand, moving to Australia with her family when she was seven, Shelley currently lives in Central Queensland, Australia, with her husband and two young children. They share their home with two wrecking ball kitties, a deformed budgerigar, and one pipsqueak of a dog that is fairly normal as dogs go.

Shelley loves to hear from her readers so feel free to contact her on Facebook or leave a review on Amazon or Goodreads or on her website - shelleyrussellnolan.com

ALSO BY SHELLEY RUSSELL NOLAN

Arcane Awakenings Books One and Two

A hidden past. An uncertain future.

In *Angel Fire*, all Andie wants is acceptance, a task made difficult thanks to the nightmare that's plagued her for the past fifteen years. Then she learns it's a terrifying memory of the night she lost her identical twin. When Angel's spirit calls to her, begging to be saved, Andie is determined to discover what really happened the night her sister died.

The story continues in *Wild Lightning*, when Celeste wakes in a mental institution with no memory of who she is or why she can shoot lightning from her fingertips. Spurred on by a vision of Angel, Celeste escapes and searches for answers as her captors close in.

Andie and Celeste must battle ruthless adversaries as they seek to uncover the truth, but will this lead to a future more dangerous than what they've left behind?

Arcane Awakenings – a fast-paced paranormal fantasy novella series.

Arcane Awakenings Books Three and Four

Freedom comes at a cost.

In *Hidden Aftershock*, after escaping from the Wood Estate and being reunited with her family, Angel is finally free to enjoy her life. But she knows it won't last. Dr Wood is still out there, determined to complete her research. When unexplained earthquakes rock Easton, and Angel's dreams point her in the direction of the Estate, she makes a decision that could end her freedom for good.

Then in *Blind Sight*, after being blinded in a car accident, Belinda begins having visions of future events. When her ability becomes public knowledge, she is targeted by a ruthless scientist. Only by joining forces with Angel and the others will Belinda have any hope of escaping the trap he sets for her.

Angel and Belinda must overcome their limitations to gain the freedom they deserve. But will the cost of that freedom prove to be too high?

Arcane Awakenings – a fast-paced paranormal fantasy novella series.

Lost Reaper
(Book One of the Reaper Series)

The first dead body I ever saw was my own.

For twenty-five year old Tyler Morgan, being murdered was easy. Easy in comparison with working for the Grim Reaper.

Jonathon Grimm may have brought her back from the dead in exchange for working as a reaper for her hometown, Easton, but she has to find his lost reaper before she can enjoy her second chance at life. Only ... the lost reaper isn't actually lost. He has a new body and a new life and no intention of turning himself in, even if it means giving Tyler her life back.

Tyler begins the grisly task of reaping the souls of Easton's dead while searching for the reaper. He could be anyone – the intriguing detective, Sam Lockwood; the handsome, wealthy Chris Bradbury; or the serial killer stalking the women of Easton. Women who bear an uncanny resemblance to Tyler.

But what is the ancient secret, hidden from mankind, that has motivated Grimm to choose Tyler for the morbid task?

As the killer closes in and Grimm's deadline draws closer, Tyler discovers she is fighting a much bigger threat than the Grim Reaper and time is running out for everyone.

Winged Reaper
(Book Two of the Reaper Series)

Secrets, lies and the Grim Reaper: a recipe for disaster!

Twenty-five-year-old Tyler Morgan is only alive--technically reborn--because the Grim Reaper offered her a job. Now she has to find a way to stop her 'boss' from starting a war that threatens the survival of mankind.

Weak and in need of fresh souls, the Grim Reaper has sent his Wraiths to Tyler's hometown, Easton, and by the time he gets his fill, it could turn into a graveyard.

Tyler's resolve is tested when old secrets surface and a new betrayal has her questioning where her loyalties lie.

Supported by the intriguing detective, Sam Lockwood; the handsome, wealthy Chris Bradbury; and sources she never expected to come to her aid, Tyler must fight her way to the truth if she is ever to find the strength to harness the powers she has inherited, and vanquish the Grim Reaper forever.

Silver Reaper
(Book Three of the Reaper Series)

How far would you go to save those marked for Death?

When the call to reap uncovers a new threat to Easton and its inhabitants, Tyler is drawn back into a world she thought she'd left behind.

Forced to face her greatest fears, she seeks to uncover the identity of the rogue reaper murdering men employed by her former ally. But the search leads her to a conspiracy decades in the making.

With the line between friends and enemies blurring, Tyler begins to question her loyalties as she fights to stop the storm threatening to engulf Easton. But when the Grim Reaper offers the last hope, death might be the least of her problems.

Who can Tyler trust when even her allies want her dead?